SOMEWHERE IN THE DARKNESS

**Other books by
Walter Dean Myers:**

*Fallen Angels
Scorpions
Motown and Didi: A Love Story
The Young Landlords
The Legend of Tarik
Fast Sam, Cool Clyde & Stuff*

SOMEWHERE IN THE
DARKNESS

WALTER DEAN MYERS

SCHOLASTIC
HARDCOVER

Scholastic Inc.
New York

Library of Congress Cataloging-in-Publication Data

Myers, Walter Dean, 1937–
  Somewhere in the darkness / Walter Dean Myers.
    p.   cm.
  Summary: A teenage boy accompanies his father, who has recently
escaped from prison, on a trip that turns out to be a time of often
painful discovery for them both.
  ISBN 0-590-42411-4
  [1. Fathers and sons — Fiction. 2. Interpersonal relations —
Fiction. 3. Prisoners — Fiction.] I. Title.
PZ7.M992So 1992
  [Fic]— —dc20   91-19295
                                                            CIP
                                                             AC

12 11 10 9 8 7 6 5 4 3   3 4 5 6 7/9

                        Printed in the U.S.A.   37

                  First Scholastic Printing, May 1992

For Paris Griffin,
a friend.

SOMEWHERE IN THE DARKNESS

Jimmy Little sat on the edge of the bed, eyes closed, listening to the rain that beat against the window. In the street below cars hissed by. From somewhere a radio blared. It had been on for most of the night. He leaned back his head and opened his eyes halfway. He looked into the mirror. The mahogany framing the oval glass was nearly the same color as his face. Jimmy smiled; he liked the way he looked in the morning.

"Jimmy?" The voice came gently through the door.

"I'm up, Mama Jean," he called.

"You don't want to be late for school today," she said. "You dressed?"

"Yeah."

The door opened and Mama Jean stuck her head in the door. Jimmy smiled.

"I do hope you don't intend going to school just dressed in your underpants," Mama Jean said.

"No, ma'am."

"There are some eggs in the refrigerator and some

1

of that ham I bought yesterday," she said. "Don't you fool around here and be late, now. You know what that teacher said."

"Yes, ma'am."

"You all right?" She came into the room and put her hand on his forehead. "You don't look too perky this morning."

"That radio was on all night," he said.

"Wasn't it?" Mama Jean opened his dresser drawer to see if he had a clean shirt. "Don't know what's wrong with those people. Now you get yourself on out of here on time today, hear?"

"I'll be out on time," Jimmy said.

Mama Jean kissed him and left his room.

He heard her shuffling about the kitchen, imagined her moving her large frame around the table, pushing a gray hair in place, straightening up some salt shaker or one of the green vases that held the flowers she loved so, before getting ready to leave for work. The keys jangled as she took them off the refrigerator.

"Don't forget to lock up good," she called to him.

"Yes, ma'am."

The door opened and shut behind her. First one lock and then the other clicked into place.

Jimmy looked at the calendar taped to his closet. Wednesday. Mama Jean would be going to take care of the Sumner baby. She had been taking care of the child since it was born, as she had taken care of its mother years earlier. Sometimes, when there wasn't any school, he would go with her over to the Sumner house. Mrs. Sumner was younger than his teacher. Taking care of the baby didn't seem that hard. Mama Jean wasn't young, but she wasn't really old, either. Not that old, anyway.

Jimmy looked out of the window, saw Mama Jean reach the corner holding her small umbrella higher than he thought she should have. It was bent on one side, but it kept the rain off. The rain was lighter than it had been, and he thought she probably wouldn't get too wet. He watched until she turned the corner. He took his pants from the back of a chair and went into the bathroom.

The cold water felt good on his face. He wet the cloth again and, leaning backward, squeezed it out over his forehead so that it ran down his face and onto his neck and shoulders. He was thinking about whether or not he would go to school. He told himself that he didn't feel like it.

"The boy has got to realize how important education is," his teacher had said to Mama Jean. "Especially for our people."

"I'm going to stay on him," Mama Jean had said.

When they got home Mama Jean had lectured him on how important reading and writing were. He hadn't answered, just listened. There was nothing to say; he knew she was right.

Jimmy shook some baking soda from the box into a glass, put a few drops of water in it, and started brushing his teeth with it.

Jimmy had managed the ninth grade fairly well, but the tenth was going badly. He hadn't figured out exactly why. Somehow things were just falling apart. It had happened before but usually he could pull things together. This year it was just harder, he told himself.

He used the toilet, finished washing up, and then went back to the bedroom to dress. He took his clothes into the living room and turned on the television. He half watched the morning news as he put on his socks. In his mind he played scenes about going to school. In one he went and Mr. Haynes met him at the door and asked where he had been.

"Sick," he answered.

"You have a note?"

He could write one and sign Mama Jean's name to it, he thought. Mama Jean would have a fit if she found out, though. She'd be hurt, too. That was the worst part, the way she would look at him and be disappointed. He decided against writing the note.

He poured out some cornflakes into a bowl. On the way to the refrigerator for the milk he turned the volume up on the television. A roach ran up the wall next to the refrigerator and behind a picture. Disgusting. Jimmy moved the picture and chased the roach.

"Hoo! Hoo!" he shouted at the roach.

The roach scurried down the wall and behind the stove. He hadn't seen a roach in the house for almost a year. He'd have to tell Mama Jean about it. She'd put out some traps.

There were streaks across the old black-and-white set. Jimmy knew they would disappear once the set warmed up.

The phone rang. He glanced at the clock. It was probably Mama Jean calling to make sure that he had gone to school. He didn't answer it.

The funny thing was that he never knew he wasn't going to school until he found that he wasn't there. Every morning he would think that he was going to school. Then he would drift down McDonough Street and turn left instead of right, or cut across Rockaway Boulevard toward Fulton. If he went down to McDonough he would end up in the playground near the projects. He would meet K.C. and Ivory and they would hang out together or go to K.C.'s house and watch television. If he went to Fulton he would just walk, sometimes all the way downtown, and daydream.

His daydreams were filled with make-believe places and make-believe people; brave knights who came from kingdoms far away to kill dragons and rescue anyone who needed rescuing. He had only spoken of his dreams once. He had taken a test and had scored high on it, higher than they had expected. As a result he had to see a psychologist who came around once a month. He thought the interview would be okay, that maybe they would tell him it was okay that he had got bad grades and that he could start all over again.

"What we're wondering," the sandy-haired man had said, "is why someone of your intelligence is doing so badly in school?"

He had shrugged, had fished about for words, and found none. The psychologist asked him questions.

"How do you get along with your mother?"

"Okay," he had answered.

"And is there a father around?"

"What you mean by that?" he had answered, annoyed.

"Oh, I just asked." The psychologist turned slightly in his chair. "There are a lot of single-parent homes in this school."

"Yeah," Jimmy said. "We get along all right."

"What kind of work does he do?"

"He works in a bus garage," Jimmy said. "He sees that all the buses are checked once a month."

"That's a good job," the psychologist said. "Your father is obviously an intelligent man, too."

Jimmy sat up in his chair. He had to listen carefully to the psychologist in case he came back with any trick questions about his father. He didn't think the psychologist believed that his father worked in a bus garage. He tried to think of other things the psychologist might ask, and to come up with answers for them.

"Do you dream much?" he asked.

"What?"

"What do you dream about?" he asked.

Maybe it was because he was thinking about questions about his father, or that he hadn't expected him to ask about dreams. But he had let his guard down, had told the man about his unicorns, and about him being a knight and rescuing a princess.

"You dream about — what was it? — unicorns? Every night?"

"I mostly think about it," Jimmy said. "I don't dream about it, you know, like at night or nothing like that."

"What do you dream about at night?"

"I don't know. I don't even know if I dream at night," Jimmy answered.

"You're a bit old to be daydreaming about imaginary creatures, aren't you?" the psychologist said.

There was the hint of a smile on the psychologist's face. Jimmy looked past him to the clock on the wall. The wall was painted green on the bottom and white at the top. The line dividing the white and green went right behind the clock. Jimmy looked back at the psychologist. He was writing on his pad. Jimmy didn't answer any more questions.

It wasn't anybody's business, he thought, that his real mother was dead. His father wasn't anybody's business, either. Neither were his daydreams. Sometimes, he thought, adults didn't like the idea of kids thinking anything or knowing anything they didn't know. Jimmy enjoyed letting his mind wander, enjoyed the thoughts that ran through his mind like a long, pleasant movie.

"You thinking enough for two or three people," Mama Jean said. "You're going to wear out your brain before you're twenty-one!"

"That means I got six more years to use it," Jimmy had answered. "That's not too bad."

He turned off the television, grabbed his composition book from the table, and left the small apartment.

There was tin on the stairs, and he made sure he landed hard on each step as he went down. He didn't want to surprise some junkie messing around on the stairs or dealing dope. Let them know he was coming.

They lived on the fourth floor of a seven-storied building. The elevator didn't work, and the owner had boarded up the stairs at the top of the fifth floor. Sometimes he could hear people going on past the fifth floor. Once a month the superintendent would get the cops to go up and chase away the junkies, but they would always come back.

When he reached the ground floor Cookie was standing in front of the mailboxes.

"You going to school?" she asked. Cookie was in

her twenties and as skinny as she could get, but she was still kind of nice-looking.

"Who you, the F.B.I.?"

"If I see you on the street I'm going to tell Mama Jean on you," she giggled.

Jimmy looked down the street. The rain had slackened even more but the streets were still wet. In the middle of the street an oil patch had about three different colors in it. Across the street Mr. Johnson sat on the sidewalk outside of Brownie's Bar.

"You waiting for the mailman?" Jimmy asked.

"Un-huh." Cookie looked down the street. "I don't know why. He ain't bringing me nothing I want."

"Then why you waiting for him?" Jimmy asked.

"Who you, the F.B.I.?"

Jimmy smiled. "Just asked," he said.

"Go on with your pretty smile," Cookie said. "If you was about four years older I'd give you a play."

"How you know I want a play?"

" 'Cause you're a man," Cookie said. "If you don't want a play now, you will in about another year. How old are you?"

"Sixteen."

"No such a lie!"

"Almost sixteen."

"Fourteen," Cookie said. "Mama Jean told me. Look at Mr. Johnson over there. I don't know why he don't catch TB or nothing."

Jimmy looked over at Mr. Johnson. He was already drunk, and now he was trying to stand. He got to one knee, put his back against a sign on the wall, and tried to slide himself to a standing position.

The sign was for Bustelo coffee, and Mr. Johnson had his shoulder right at the B.

"I got to get on to school," Jimmy said.

"You want to borrow an umbrella?"

"You got one?"

"No, I asked if you wanted to borrow one 'cause I haven't got none and my lips needed some exercise," Cookie said, shaking her head. "C'mon and get it."

He followed Cookie down the hall to her first-floor apartment. He had been in Cookie's house before. Sometimes he went to the store for her and if he did she would always give him soda and potato chips or whatever she had.

The apartment smelled like talcum powder and furniture polish. Jimmy didn't mind the talcum powder, he didn't even mind when Cookie's baby made a mess and stunk up the place, but he hated the smell of furniture polish.

Cookie's television was on, and he watched it as she looked for her umbrella. A woman was talking about how some singer was making a comeback. Then they showed a few seconds of the singer in a nightclub. Jimmy looked at him and he didn't look very old.

"I'm going over to Nancy's," Cookie said. "I think I loaned her my umbrella."

"I don't need it," Jimmy said.

"Why should you go out there and get wet?" Cookie asked. "Keep an eye on Kwame while I run over to Nancy's and get my umbrella."

"Don't stay a long time," Jimmy said. "I don't want to get to school too late."

Cookie left, and Jimmy looked at Kwame sleeping in a corner of the crib. He went to the top of the crib and looked down at the baby. There was a pacifier in his mouth, and Jimmy reached in and took it out. Mama Jean said that if a baby slept with a pacifier in its mouth its teeth would grow crooked.

Kwame moved one leg, and then Jimmy saw him making sucking motions with his mouth. He was about to put the pacifier back in when Kwame stopped moving.

Jimmy sat down and watched the rest of the television program.

$\mathbf{C}$ookie came back with an umbrella, a small red one that Jimmy wouldn't have carried across the street, let alone to the school.

"She couldn't find my umbrella," Cookie said. "She had this piece of thing. You want to take it?"

"That's okay," Jimmy answered. "It's not raining that hard."

Cookie said something about him thinking he was too much of a man to carry a red umbrella but he saw that she was disappointed that Nancy didn't have her umbrella.

"You gonna get soaked if the rain picks up," she said.

"Then I'll come in here and make you fix me some tea," he said. He pulled his jacket up around his collar.

"Drop by when you get home," she said.

When he reached the doorway the rain had just about stopped but it was cold and windy. Bits of paper flew down the street, in between parked cars, slapping against the legs of early-morning workers hurrying toward the subway. Across the street some little boys were standing around Mr. Johnson. The neighborhood drunk was leaning against a building, going through his pockets looking for whatever he thought he had there.

Jimmy was already late for school. But he was trying to figure out a strategy. He needed to know what to do, how to get things together to get him through the year. It was March, and he only had a few months to go. If he could get it all together just one more time, just for a few months, he could get out of the tenth grade and then maybe be straight for the eleventh. He was way behind, but he knew that some of the other kids didn't have any more than he did going for them. Only they didn't have a bad attendance record. That was what they got you on. You could do bad in school and maybe still get by if most of the other kids messed up, too. But the attendance record was different. They'd get you on that and leave you back in a minute.

The wind was in his face as he leaned forward into it. Already the familiar smells of garlic and fried plantains was in the air. An old, bowlegged man stood in the doorway of the Muslim shop with his chess board under his arm.

A sharp cry came from behind him and he turned. A kid had thrown something at Mr. Johnson. The drunk, partially crippled, waved at them with his good hand and ranted. Jimmy turned on his heel and went back to the small crowd.

"Yo, y'all get on out of here and leave him alone!" he called out.

"Who you?" A defiant little boy, Jimmy figured

he couldn't have been more than nine, stepped forward.

"I'm the guy that's gonna kick your little butt!" Jimmy said, pushing the boy back with his body.

The boy looked at Jimmy sullenly, then backed off. The other kids started off, looking for an amusement other than Mr. Johnson.

"They ain't got no respect," Mr. Johnson said.

Jimmy shrugged.

The school was on McDonough and Gates. There was a police car sitting in front of it when he arrived. Inside the car two policemen were having coffee.

"You know what time it is?" Mr. Haynes called out from the top of the stairs. He had a radio in his hand. "And when's the last time you were in school?"

"My mother called the nurse," Jimmy said.

"You got a doctor's note?"

"I told you my mother called the nurse," Jimmy said, trying to walk past the assistant principal.

Mr. Haynes put one broad hand in front of Jimmy's chest to stop him and pointed toward the detention office. "You wait for me in there."

Jimmy thought about turning around and leaving the school, then went into the detention office. There were four other boys there and two girls.

"We all got to go home." Randy Johnson was sitting in a corner eating a sandwich.

"I don't care," Jimmy said.

"I didn't even do nothing," Rosalind Epps said. The big girl sprawled out over half the bench. "I don't even know why I'm in here."

"You were late," Jimmy said.

"No, I wasn't!" Rosalind said.

"She wasn't late," Randy said. "Mr. Haynes just picked me and her out and told us to come in here. We was the first ones in here and we was on time and everything."

Jimmy didn't believe them, but he didn't say anything. There wasn't any reason for them being in the detention room if they were on time.

Mr. Haynes came into the detention room with three more kids. Then he passed around the detention sheet and everybody had to sign it.

"What you do?" Rosalind asked the light-skinned boy that had come in with Mr. Haynes.

"I didn't do nothing," was the answer. "I just got picked. I think we got to carry some supplies or something. 'Cause he just asked the teacher something and she sent me down here with him."

Outside the rain was picking up again. It splattered against the window, making patterns against the dirt-frosted glass.

Mr. Haynes got the detention sheet and took it into the inner office.

"What I *do*?" Rosalind called after him.

Mr. Haynes shut the door.

"Where you been?" Maurice Douglass stuck his head in the door. "I thought you dropped out, man."

"Been busy," Jimmy said to his friend.

"You hear that Tony 'D' cut Billy?"

"Basketball Billy?" Jimmy asked.

"Yeah, he was messing with him in the lunchroom and Tony 'D' cut him."

"They had cops all over the place," Rosalind added. "They was searching people's lockers and everything. They didn't have no right to go through all that just because one guy cut a dude."

Mr. Haynes stuck his head out of the door. "Maurice, get upstairs to your class!"

"Yes, sir, Mr. Boss Man." Maurice made a ceremonious bow and left.

"Jimmy, you go on up to your classroom. Everybody else shut up and be quiet until I get to you."

"How come he get to go upstairs when he come in late? I seen him when he come in!" Rosalind was saying as Jimmy went out the door.

He thought that Rosalind had probably done something the day before. Maybe when they had searched the lockers they had found something in her locker. He caught up with Maurice and asked when the cutting had taken place.

"Day before yesterday," Maurice said. "But check this out. Tony just nicked the dude and he was screaming and carrying on like he had stabbed him through the heart or something."

"No lie?"

"Yeah, hey, look, you want to play some ball tonight?"

"I don't know."

"You give up ball or something, man?" Maurice looked at him sideways. "We playing Richie and his crew."

"I'll see how I'm feeling," Jimmy said.

"You ain't going to play," Maurice said. "You getting to be another jive dude, man."

Jimmy went into his classroom. Miss Cumberbatch was standing in front of the class, and everybody was sitting quietly. He tried not to look at her. All the desks were clear, and he put his notebook on the floor.

"We're taking achievement tests today," Miss
Cumberbatch said.

Bet. Now Jimmy realized why Rosalind was down
in the office. They were snatching out the kids who
were going to really mess up on the tests. They knew
he wasn't going to mess up and that's why they let
him up in the classroom. That was good, he thought.
Maybe by the next day they would have forgotten
that he hadn't been in school that week.

The test was hard. It had four parts, two English
and two math. The math part was easier than the
English.

Halfway through the tests he remembered that
he hadn't brought any lunch money. He felt his
pockets to see if he had anything left over from the
day before. Nothing. He'd have to borrow somebody's lunch card and hope that nobody stupid was
on the door.

The test was over fifteen minutes before lunch,
but Miss Cumberbatch said that the class was dis-
missed for the day.

"Anybody who wants to go to lunch can," she said.
"But you don't have to."

He thought about going to lunch because he was
hungry. He saw Maurice and Chris Clarke standing
in the hallway near the lunchroom. They were probably looking for guys to play ball. He didn't want to
play. He could have borrowed some sneakers but
he thought he'd go on home.

"Hey, Shirley, how you doing?"

"And just where have you been, Jimmy Little?"
Shirley was one of those girls who always did well.
She was tall, almost as tall as he was, and went to
the same church.

"I've been sick," he lied.

"You don't look sick to me," she said.

"Why don't you let me borrow your notebook so I can catch up with some of the work?" he asked.

"We haven't been doing anything for the last few days except reviewing for these tests," Shirley said. "What was wrong with you?"

"Just sick," Jimmy said. "Didn't get to the doctors. Maybe I'll go this afternoon."

"You coming to school tomorrow?"

"If I ain't got nothing too bad." Jimmy smiled.

"Later, sickey." Shirley waved her hand at him and went on down the hall.

Jimmy hadn't been sick so much as he had been tired. It was a funny kind of tired, not the kind that you got from playing ball. No muscles ached, his arms and legs weren't tired. It seemed to come from inside. It was almost as if something tired was growing in him. In the mornings he would just get up and not feel like doing anything. He didn't know why.

One morning, after Mama Jean had left, he tried to concentrate on each part of his body to see if that part was okay. He thought about his feet first and worked his way up. Nothing hurt. Nothing seemed particularly out of sorts, but nothing seemed to work. It was an effort just to walk around the house.

Television helped. Television was kind of doing something when he wasn't doing anything. He could sit and watch the movies, watch old *I Love Lucy* shows or movies where nobody seemed to know anything. Everything surprised them, and people who were watching the movies knew what the people in the movies should have known. When a movie was like that it seemed as if you were a part of it.

He wished he had gotten Shirley's notebook anyway. He had said that he wanted to see what he had missed, but he hadn't taken a lot of notes even when he was going to school most of the time.

Mr. Johnson was lying on the ground in front of his building. If he didn't get himself up before the little kids got out of school he was going to be in big trouble. The little kids didn't know anything about how to be. They would play with a drunk the same way they would play with an old ball they found.

"Jimmy! Come here, quick!" Cookie was in the doorway.

"What?"

"There was a guy here looking for you," Cookie said. "A tall guy. Said he knew you. I haven't seen him around here before."

"How early?" Jimmy asked.

"Just a little bit after you left," Cookie said.

"He put anything in the mailbox?"

"I think he still up there."

"Up where?" Jimmy asked.

"Upstairs," Cookie said. "I didn't see him coming down. I went in and checked on Kwame for about a minute but that was all."

"He's probably from the school," Jimmy said. "No big deal."

"You still want that tea?" Cookie asked, relieved that Jimmy didn't think the guy looking for him was anything special.

"Maybe later," Jimmy said. "You seen Mama Jean?"

"No."

"I'll see you later," Jimmy said.

He went up the stairs quickly. They only had one mailbox key, which Mama Jean kept on the top of the refrigerator. If a guy came from the school they might have sent a note, too, Jimmy thought.

He got to the fourth floor, fumbled through his pockets until he found the key, and opened the door slowly If Mama Jean was tired, maybe she had forgot to look in the mailbox.

"Mama Jean!" he called out.

There was no answer.

"Mama Jean?" he looked in her bedroom. It was empty. He went into the kitchen, found the mailbox key in the basket on the refrigerator, and went back downstairs. He took the stairs three at a time. He opened the mailbox. There were three pieces of mail: a postcard from Herbert Jewelers, a bill from the electric company, and an advertisement from Macy's. There was nothing from the school.

"How you doing!"

The voice startled Jimmy. He turned to see a tall, thin man leaning against the wall.

"Doing okay," Jimmy said, trying to lower his voice so he would seem older.

"Your name is Little, isn't it?" the man asked.

"Yeah," Jimmy said. "Who you?"

"I'm your father," the man replied.

The man was tall and so thin that Jimmy could see the outline of his shoulder bones through the dark green shirt he wore. He had an odd way of holding his head down and looking up at Jimmy. Jimmy opened his mouth so that the man in front of him couldn't tell how quickly he was breathing. He moved the key away from the mailbox.

"I know you don't remember me," the man said. His voice was flat and low so that Jimmy had to strain to hear him.

"How you doing?" Jimmy asked. The words came out higher than he wanted them to.

"I guess I'm doing okay," he said. "You sure got big."

"What's my name?" Jimmy asked.

"Your name is Jimmy."

"It's really James," Jimmy said.

"No, it's not," the man said. "It's Jimmy, because that was your mother's brother's name. That's who you named after."

"I thought . . ." Jimmy searched for the words. "Mama Jean said you were . . . away."

"I'm out now," the man said.

"You want to go upstairs?"

The man smiled. "How I know you really my boy?" he said. "You might be some kind of stick-up man who gets people in their apartment and then takes their money."

"You the one that said you were my father," Jimmy said.

"You remember my name?"

"What is it?"

"It's really Cephus, but that ain't what they call me."

"Crab?"

The man nodded, and Jimmy thought that there, in the light slanting down from the window, he saw a glistening in the man's eyes before he turned away. In a moment he had turned back toward Jimmy. "I guess we can go up and sit down for a while."

Jimmy wasn't sure. The man knew his father's name, even what people called him, but he didn't look like the picture in Mama Jean's album. He was skinny, he could have been a crack head.

"You scared to let me inside," the man said, leaning against the banister. "It's okay. We can wait for Jean to come home."

Jimmy went up the stairs first. He didn't know what to think. In a way he was afraid, but he wasn't sure why. Mama Jean had told him that his father was in jail. She hadn't said anything about him coming out any time soon. When they reached the apartment Jimmy thought about what he would do if the man wasn't his father and tried to do something. He walked funny; Jimmy thought he could probably outrun the guy.

He unlocked the door and opened it. The man walked away, and for a moment Jimmy thought he was leaving, but then he picked up a jacket and a package from the stairs that Jimmy hadn't noticed before and came back to the door.

"You were up here before?" Jimmy asked.

"A while ago," the man said.

Jimmy stood aside and let him in. He walked in and looked around and nodded approvingly.

"When you get out?"

"Last week," the man said. "Took me a while to figure out what I wanted to do. Got any coffee or anything?"

"I can make some," Jimmy said. "I got to put my books away first."

"Yeah, okay." The man sat down on a kitchen chair next to the table and stretched his legs out in front of him.

Jimmy went into Mama Jean's bedroom, looked under the Bible stand, and found her photo album. He turned the pages as quickly as he could, past the picture in the soldier's uniform because it was too dark, then found the one he was looking for.

In the picture was a tall, well-built man leaning against a car. There was a woman standing next to him and next to the woman was Mama Jean. The woman in between was his mother.

The man in the picture didn't look much like the man in the other room except for the wide forehead and the way he was tilting his head forward and looking up out of the picture.

"It look like me?"

Jimmy jumped and slammed the book shut.

"Let's see it," the man said.

Jimmy looked through the book again, slowly, until he found the picture. Then he showed it to the man.

"Me and your mama were thinking about buying a car," the man said, holding up the album. "We went up to the Bronx and looked at some and figured out how much we were going to need for a down payment. We were talking about getting it up, I think it was a hundred dollars, something like that. It wasn't real talk because we didn't have no hundred dollars to be putting out. Dolly told Jean and Jean said maybe we could all buy a car together. Jean and your mama were tight, real tight."

"You buy the car?"

"No, we got our piece of the money together and then your mama wanted to buy a living room set and that was that. You know how a woman can get with that kind of thing."

Jimmy looked at the picture again, then went into the kitchen.

He found the pot and started spooning coffee into the basket.

"How come you didn't write and let everybody know you were coming?" he asked as he ran tap water into the pot.

"Didn't know what I wanted to do," Crab said. He took out a handkerchief, coughed into it, and then spit into it.

"There's some Kleenex on the counter," Jimmy said.

"I didn't think you were going to be so big," Crab

said. "You know, I had this thing in my head that I was going see you and pick you up and put you on top of the refrigerator. You imagine me trying to pick you up and put you on the refrigerator?"

"Put me on what . . .?" Even as he said the words an image came to him, of him looking down from the refrigerator and reaching for somebody.

"I used to do that when you were a kid," the man said.

"Oh."

"How you doing in school and everything?"

"Okay." Jimmy finished putting the water in the coffeepot and put it on the stove. He looked over at the man and saw him watching him. "Sometimes I make coffee for Mama Jean," he said.

"You fourteen, now?"

"Almost fifteen," Jimmy said. "In a couple of months."

"Yeah, okay."

"So now you decided what you going to do?" Jimmy turned down the flame until it was an even glow under the battered aluminum pot.

"Yeah," the man said. "I thought you and me might go around the country a bit."

A knock came on the door, and the man froze for a moment, then held his hand up to Jimmy. "I want to surprise Jean," he said.

He stood up quickly and went into the next room. The move scared Jimmy. He watched the door close and then open slightly. The knock came on the door again.

"Who is it?" Jimmy called.

"Cookie."

Jimmy opened the door.

"Was the guy from school here?" Cookie asked. She relaxed in the framework of the door so that one hip jutted out.

"No, that was just somebody I know," Jimmy said.

"Oh." Cookie nodded. "Tell Mama Jean I'm making some collard greens and if she want some to send you downstairs to get them, okay?"

"Yeah."

"Jimmy, don't get to watching television and forgetting to tell Mama Jean 'cause I spent all afternoon cleaning them collard greens," Cookie said.

"I'm not going to forget," Jimmy said.

Cookie shook her finger at him and started for the stairs.

"Maybe I shouldn't surprise Jean," the man said when Jimmy had closed the door.

"She don't like surprises," Jimmy said. "Especially when they scare her or something."

"Yeah, you right," the man said.

"What you mean, go around the country?" Jimmy asked.

"You know where I been, right?"

"Yeah."

"Well, I sit up there and figured what you must be thinking about me. You know what I mean?"

"I wasn't thinking nothing about you," Jimmy said. He got some bread from a loaf, buttered two slices, and put them in the oven. "We got some jelly and stuff, you want that?"

"Yeah, that's okay."

Jimmy got the jelly out of the refrigerator.

"The way I figure, if it was my father that was in

jail I would think something about him," the man said. "People must have told you some terrible stuff about me."

Sometimes, when Jimmy was alone, he would think of what Mama Jean had told him. There had been a holdup, and some men had been killed. He had imagined his father standing there, legs apart, holding a gun and shooting people.

"Mama Jean just said you needed the money and you made a mistake," Jimmy said.

"What kind of mistake?"

"Shooting people and stuff." Jimmy looked at him.

"Suppose I told you I didn't do it?" he said. "You believe me?"

"You say so I guess I do," Jimmy said. Jimmy went to the window and looked down to the street. A dog, soaked from the rain, moved up against the building. Its tail was between its legs and it shied away from two small kids walking down the street.

"You think I really didn't do it or you think I'm just saying it?"

"Everybody say they didn't do nothing," Jimmy said. "They just ain't going to put you in jail for nothing."

"That's why I come here," he said. " 'Cause I figure you got to be believing that I went out here and killed somebody. You don't know what to think about me. You don't even know what to call me."

"What you mean?"

"What you call that girl that was here a little while ago?"

"Cookie?"

"You call her by her name. And I hear you talking

about Mama Jean. What you think you should call me?"

Jimmy looked at him and looked back down into the street again. He was sorry he had let him into the house.

"So what I'm supposed to call you?"

"You can call me Crab," he said. "I thought about it, and that's what my friends call me. Maybe we can get to be friends. What you think?"

Mama Jean was walking down the street. Jimmy didn't say anything.

The coffee started perking, and Jimmy turned it down more. It stopped perking and he checked the light to make sure it hadn't gone completely out. It hadn't, and soon the coffee was perking again. He wondered if there was any milk in the refrigerator, checked, and saw that there was.

Jimmy thought about going downstairs and telling Mama Jean about the guy. He wished he knew some sure thing to do.

"So you call me Crab and I'll call you Jimmy," Crab continued. "That's okay with you?"

"Okay," Jimmy answered.

"You know I got a lot of things to say to you about being sorry about not writing and stuff like that."

"You can write anytime you want to when you in jail?"

"Yeah, that's about all you can do anytime you want to," Crab said. "I did write you a couple of letters but I didn't mail any of them."

"How come?"

"Didn't know what to say most of the time," Crab said. "Then when I wrote down what I wanted to say it didn't sound right. You know, you got to ease

on in to some things. You can't just bust it out because you think it's right."

Jimmy would have liked to look at him good without him looking back. He would have liked to stand
them both up in front of a mirror and see how they
looked together. But he knew that he was looking
at him, watching every move he made. He couldn't
relax.

"So you glad you out, huh?"

"Yeah, I'm glad. You got to be glad to get out,"
Crab said. "It's no place to spend your life, in no
jail. That's worse than being a slave."

"My friend said they got a lot of Muslims in jail."

"They got a lot of different kinds of religion," Crab
said. "People got a lot of time to think about what
they're all about. You know, you sit in jail with all
that time and you start doing the thinking you should
have done a long time ago."

Jimmy got two cups down and put them on the
table.

"You drink a lot of coffee?" Crab asked.

"Unh-uh. Mama Jean coming. I don't think you
should jump out at her or nothing," Jimmy said.

"She coming now?"

"Yeah." Jimmy heard the stairs creak and went
to the door. He glanced back at Crab. He had tensed
again. He sat up and took the cup in both hands.

He opened the door before Mama Jean knocked.

"I hope you didn't see me coming down the street
when we needed milk or something, boy." Mama
Jean had a shopping bag with celery sticking out of
one side.

"Crab's here," Jimmy said.

"Who?" Mama Jean stopped in the doorway, then

looked at Crab. "Well, I'll be . . . ! When did you get here, man?"

" 'Bout two hours ago." Crab stood and went around the table and put his arms around Mama Jean.

"Oh, my goodness!" Mama Jean leaned back. "Let me look at you! Oh, my goodness!"

Jimmy watched as the two hugged. Mama Jean was shaking her head and patting Crab on his shoulder.

"When did you get out? Child, we got to have a party or something! You know Sonny still living down the street? Did you call him?"

"No." Crab shook his head. "I can't stay. I got a job offer out in Chicago and I got to take it. I just come by to pick up Jimmy."

"What?" Mama Jean went to a chair and sat down heavily. She looked at Crab and then at Jimmy, then turned back to Crab. "Oh, no, Crab, don't tell me you got to take Jimmy away from me."

"I got to take the job, Jean," Crab said. "That's one of the conditions of my being released."

"Well, can't he wait until . . . " Mama Jean stood and grabbed Crab again and started to hug him. "We can talk about it later, tomorrow or sometime. Just let me look at you!"

"I got to go tonight," Crab said.

Mama Jean took a deep breath and straightened up. Jimmy saw the corners of her mouth tighten as she looked at Crab. The big woman turned and went over to the sink and turned on the water. She started washing her hands and humming.

"I been in jail for almost nine years," Crab said. "I can't do nothing they don't want me to do and get myself back in again. If they want me working by the end of the week I got to be working. That's all there is to it."

Mama Jean kept on humming. A bus passed in the street below, the low moaning of its engine seeming to answer Mama Jean's humming.

"You got to work in Chicago?" Jimmy asked.

"I should have been on the way to Chicago now," Crab said, twisting in the chair until he faced away from Jimmy. "The bus takes forever to get there. I just figured that once I got on the job the man wasn't going to let me just take off and come here and get the boy."

"Oh." Jimmy looked over at Mama Jean's back. Her shoulders lifted and sank with her breathing as she wiped off the countertop.

"What you think, Jean?"

"The sink's stopped up again," Mama Jean said. "That super supposed to be fixing it but it keeps getting stopped up."

"You got any tools?" Crab asked.

Mama Jean opened a drawer, pulled out an adjustable wrench, and put it on the counter. "Don't be getting water all over the floor," she said.

Crab got down on the floor in front of the sink and peered in. There were rags and some roach poison on the shelf in the door and he took them out and put them on the floor.

Mama Jean sat at the table and looked over at Jimmy. When Jimmy looked at her, tried to read her face to see what she was thinking, she looked away.

"This is an old sink," Crab was saying.

"If you can't fix it, I'll get the super in the morning," Mama Jean said.

"Just got to take the trap off," Crab said.

Jimmy watched as Crab adjusted the wrench to the nut on the bottom of the trap. The first time he tried to turn the nut the wrench slipped and went into the side of the cabinet and he swore under his breath. Jimmy looked at Mama Jean again. Her mouth was tight now.

The wind was picking up, rattling the loose panes in the window. Jimmy wondered what he would do.

"You fixing to stay in Chicago?" Mama Jean asked.

"Not if I can help it," Crab said. He turned and

looked at Mama Jean. Sweat glistened on his forehead and he wiped at his brow with his fingertips.
"Never did like Chicago."

"Then why you going there to work?"

"Wrote a lot of letters looking for a job," Crab
said. He was sitting cross-legged on the floor, bent
forward. "Most of the times I didn't even get an
answer. So when I got one I could take to the Parole
Board I took it right away. If you wait more than
three months they don't count the job offer. They
figure it might be gone."

He started easing off the nut at the bottom of the
trap. When it was loose he looked around and then
asked Jimmy if they didn't have an old can or something to catch the water in.

"Get the grease can," Mama Jean said. "Ain't
nothing much in it."

Jimmy opened the door to the freezer and got the
coffee can that Mama Jean collected grease in. She
was right, there wasn't much grease in the can, just
a little at the bottom. He gave the can to Crab.

"So I guess I won't be seeing him no more, huh?"
Mama Jean said.

Something cold grabbed at Jimmy's stomach and
twisted hard. He looked at Mama Jean and then at
Crab. Crab had his face toward the sink. From
where he stood Jimmy watched as Crab undid the
last few turns of the nut with his fingers. The water
started out; some of it ran down onto Crab's arm
before he could get the can under it. The can filled
quickly and overflowed some.

Crab put the can down and wiped up the water
that had spilled on the bottom of the cabinet.

"Jean, I want to get a job and get myself settled," he said as he finished wiping up the water. He turned and leaned on one arm. "You've cared for Jimmy all this time, I sure hope you don't think I'm just taking him away from you."

"You're going to Chicago." The voice was flat, hard-edged.

"I need to be with the boy a while," Crab said. He looked over at Jimmy. "I need to have a family for a while. When I get myself together, you know, get some of the pieces together, then maybe I can get us all together."

"I don't need you to get me together," Mama Jean said. "And I don't need you to get Jimmy together."

"I know that," Crab said. He wiped his hands with the rag he had used to clean up the water. "I'm not a fool. I know I'm talking about what I need."

"How long it gonna be before you get yourself together?" Mama Jean asked.

"I don't know," Crab said. "But soon's I do I can start thinking about moving back to New York. Then I'll find a place around here for me and Jimmy or he can stay with you."

"Suppose you don't get yourself together?" Mama Jean asked.

"Then I'll let Jimmy come back here. Get him a ticket on the train or a plane. I'm not about hurting the boy now. You know that's not me."

Crab pushed his fingers into the bottom of the trap, felt around as if he were looking for something, then pulled out a fork. There was hair entwined around the bottom of it and it was slightly bent.

"Let's see that fork," Mama Jean said.

Jimmy got it and showed it to Mama Jean. "I don't even remember seeing that fork," Jimmy said, his voice sounding strange to him.

Mama Jean looked up at him and patted him on his hand. "Crab, if you don't treat this boy right, I'm coming after you."

"He's my son, Jean," Crab said.

"Why don't you go in the morning?"

"I just can't show up late for that job," Crab said.

"Let me fix something to eat," Mama Jean said.

Jimmy's stomach was hurting awfully bad. He went into his room and started looking at his schoolbooks. The words blurred in front of him. Outside he could hear Mama Jean and Crab talking. Mama Jean was saying things like how Crab shouldn't let him get into any trouble and Crab was saying that he wouldn't. Jimmy's stomach was hurting and he was having trouble breathing. He remembered his asthma attacks when he was little. He used to stand up when they started because he thought he would die if he was lying down.

Mama Jean came into the room. He turned and looked at her. She was taking a suitcase out of his closet.

"Mama Jean?"

"Yeah?" She didn't look at him. He looked in the mirror on his dresser and saw the tears streaking down her dark face.

"You think I got to go?"

"He's your father," she said. She tightened her mouth against the sobs welling in her throat. "It's just too sudden for me to think about."

"You think I got to go?" Jimmy said again.

Mama Jean went to him and pulled his head

against her bosom. "You go with him, child," she said. "But you know you always got a home here with Mama Jean. Things go bad for you, I want you to come right back here. And if you can't get here, I'll get to wherever you are. You understand that?"

She cupped his head in her hand and looked at him. Her mouth was twisted and her face tear-streaked. Jimmy grabbed Mama Jean around her waist and held onto her as tightly as he could.

She pushed him away from her and looked into his eyes. "You understand me, honey?" she said. "As long as I have breath in this body, you have a home with me. Do you understand that?"

"I understand, Mama Jean."

Jimmy sat in the corner looking out of the window as Mama Jean packed his bag. It was all too sudden. He didn't know what to think, or how to think. Mama Jean came over to him and wiped his face with the edge of the bedspread. She forced a smile through her tears.

"We've been strong all these years," she said. "We'll still be strong, won't we?"

Jimmy nodded. Whenever things went wrong for them, Mama Jean always said the same thing. They would be strong. And so far they had been.

Mama Jean made fried chicken, Spanish rice, and went down and got some of the collard greens that Cookie had made. Cookie came up with her; Jimmy figured it was to take a look at Crab, but she didn't stay long.

They ate in silence and afterwards, when Jimmy went to wash the dishes, Mama Jean stopped him. Jimmy and Crab just sat around the table while Mama Jean finished packing Jimmy's things.

Jimmy felt bad. He didn't know what to say or whether he should even go. He could just run out into the street and stay away until Crab had left, he thought. Mama Jean had said he could come back if things didn't work out, and that was good.

"You want to take your schoolbooks?" Mama Jean asked.

Jimmy nodded. Mama Jean took the books from the telephone stand and put them into the suitcase. When she closed it Crab stood up and said it was time for them to go.

"It's going to be okay, Jimmy," he said.

When it was time to go Crab hugged Mama Jean and then Jimmy went to her. They hugged and she kissed him, and then he walked down the steps after Crab as Mama Jean looked away.

Some guys were sitting on the stoop playing tapes when Crab and Jimmy reached the front steps. They started down the street when they heard Mama Jean calling. Jimmy stopped and looked up at the window.

"Here's another book!" she called down.

"You need it?" Crab asked.

"Yeah," Jimmy said, putting down the suitcase.

He went to the stoop and held out his hands for her to throw the book. She beckoned for him to come up and get it, then disappeared into the window.

Jimmy looked at Crab, who had come up to him.

"She just can't let you go," Crab said. His voice was harder. "Come on now or she'll have you here all night."

"I'll just be a minute," Jimmy said.

He didn't wait for an answer as he bolted up the

stairs. Mama Jean was waiting for him with the book in her hand.

"Here's fifty dollars," she said, giving him the money tied up in a handkerchief. "Don't let him know you got it. Things don't go right for you, honey, you come on home."

"I can't take your money, Mama Jean."

"God is going to look out for us, Jimmy," Mama Jean said. "So don't you worry."

Mama Jean pushed him away from her, turned, and quickly went into the small apartment that was the only home he could ever remember.

Jimmy put the money in his pocket and went slowly downstairs to join Crab.

They went two blocks down the street and Crab wanted to stop for cigarettes.

"Stay here for a moment," he said to Jimmy. Jimmy watched him go toward the small bodega where Johnny Cruz's father worked. Jimmy noticed that Crab walked funny. It was as if he couldn't bend his legs good and had to walk with them stiff, swinging them slightly as he moved, his head going from side to side.

Crab went into the bodega and reappeared a moment later. He stopped and took out a cigarette and slowly lit it. Jimmy wondered if he was changing his mind about taking him to Chicago.

"You ready?" Crab asked.

"Yeah," Jimmy said.

Crab walked over to a gray Dodge, fished through his pockets, and opened the trunk.

"I didn't know you had a car," Jimmy said. "I thought you told Mama Jean we were going to take the bus."

"My driving isn't that good," he said, grinning. "She had to know that if I was in the slam all this time I wasn't practicing my driving that much. She just would have been worried about you more."

Jimmy put his bag in the trunk. Crab closed it and went around to the driver's side, opened the door, and slid in. Jimmy looked back toward where he knew Mama Jean was. He halfway expected to see her down the street, waving her arms for him to come back. If she had been there, calling to him, he might have gone back, too.

"I guess you were really surprised to see me," Crab said.

"Yeah."

"Mama Jean ever tell you to write to me?"

"She said I could if I wanted to," Jimmy said. "I don't write much."

The rain started again. Jimmy thought of Mama Jean sitting in the big chair in front of the television set, her fingertips tracing the pattern on the seat covers. Crab was fooling around with the knobs on the left side of the car, then found one that turned on the windshield wipers.

"You look like your mama," Crab said. "Something like her, anyway."

"I got the pictures of her," Jimmy said.

"I wanted to take one of them," Crab said. "Somebody stole the pictures I had of her."

"They stole the pictures?" Jimmy asked.

Crab looked at him and shrugged. "Yeah, they did. Guys ain't got no woman on the outside, they pretend they got one. Some guys cut out pictures of women in magazines. Sometimes they steal guys' pictures. Jail ain't no place to be."

As the miles went by, Jimmy began to relax a little. He was still having trouble breathing but he didn't think he was going to have an asthma attack. He knew he was tired, really tired. Once he fell asleep, only to wake with a start. Crab glanced over at him and then turned his eyes back toward the road.

Jimmy thought of Mama Jean again. He wondered if the rain would bother her arthritis. If it did she'd have trouble getting up in the morning and he wouldn't be there to make tea for her. He wondered if she were thinking about him, and if she were sad. He thought a "hello" to her, and "I love you."

He felt his eyes misting up and closed them. Things would work out okay, he told himself. He had often wondered what it would be like to have a father, like some kids. For some reason he had always imagined a father as somebody who told him to come home at a certain time or who got mad when he didn't do his homework. He had imagined them going to baseball games together or maybe for walks in the park. He hadn't thought about Chicago.

When Jimmy opened his eyes he didn't know where he was. The car was stopped at the side of the road. It was night. Up the road there were tall poles that stretched over the road like alien giraffes, their great shiny eyes lighting up the night. Jimmy could see small insects flying through the green halos around the lights on the poles. Jimmy looked over to see if Crab was in the backseat. He wasn't.

He closed his eyes again, deciding to go back to sleep. His eyes opened again almost immediately and he twisted around to look behind the car. In the distance he could see a filling station. Maybe, he thought, they had run out of gas. He got out of the car.

The night was cool, and he shivered. He walked to the back of the car and looked toward the filling station. He didn't see Crab. Something, leaves blowing across the road, a small animal, made a swishing sound in the darkness. Jimmy got back into the car and slammed the door shut. He reached for the radio, stopped, and put his hands in his lap.

He locked his door and looked to see if Crab's side was locked. It wasn't. He took a deep breath and looked back toward the filling station again.

He saw him. He could tell the tall silhouette was Crab by the way it moved. Jimmy watched as he neared, watched until the light showed enough of the older man to push away his last doubts. It was Crab, all right.

He turned, unlocked his door, and slipped down in his seat. Moments later Crab opened the door on the driver's side, slipped behind the wheel, and started the car. Jimmy kept his eyes closed as the car crunched over the gravel on the shoulder of the road, then lurched forward onto the highway. He opened his eyes and stretched.

"You awake?" Crab asked.

"Yeah," Jimmy said. "We near Chicago yet?"

"Got a way to go," Crab said. "We got to stop and get some gas soon. Maybe find a place to eat. You hungry?"

"Not that hungry," Jimmy said.

"I want to call Mama Jean, too," Crab said.

They drove in silence for another hour. In the distance the sky was beginning to lighten. They were nearing a city, and the buildings loomed against the gray sky. The traffic was picking up, and large trucks rumbled past them into the city.

"Where are we now?" Jimmy asked.

"Cleveland," Crab said.

Crab drove around for a while as if he were looking for some place, then pulled into a service station. He rolled the window down and told the attendant to fill the tank.

"Look, we're on the way to L.A. and need to get

us something to eat," Crab spoke to the brown-faced man pumping gas as if he knew him. "Can we leave the car over there against the fence while we run and get some breakfast?"

"You got to pay for the gas first," the attendant said, looking at Crab from the corners of his eyes.

"Sure, I just don't want to spend all morning looking for a parking space," Crab said, nodding.

The attendant returned the nod, and then turned his attention back to the pump. When the tank was filled Crab paid the man, then put the car over near the fence.

"Should have taken some of Mama Jean's chicken with us," Crab said as they walked across to the small diner. There was a sign over the diner that read COLONETTE.

They sat in a booth and Crab told Jimmy to order anything he wanted. Jimmy ordered pancakes and milk.

"Give me two over easy and about five pieces of bacon," Crab said.

"You only get four pieces of bacon," the man taking the order said. "You want any more than that you can pay for a double order."

"Then give me a double order and some coffee," Crab said. "Where's your phone?"

The man pointed toward the back to a wall phone, and Crab slipped out of the booth and headed for it.

Jimmy wondered what Crab had done back at the service station they had stopped at on the road. Maybe he had just gone to the bathroom, Jimmy thought.

Jimmy looked over at Crab. He had his back toward the restaurant and had his head down. He turned and looked back at Jimmy and gave him the thumbs-up sign. Jimmy gave him the thumbs-up sign back.

He wondered how he looked to Crab. Whether Crab thought that they looked alike or not. Some more people came into the diner. They were working people and mostly black. One man was tall with a long neck. He wore a belt with tools on it. Jimmy tried to figure out what he did. There were three different kinds of pliers on the broad leather belt he wore, all with red handles, a few screwdrivers, and one tool that Jimmy had never seen before. The man straddled a stool as if it were a horse and started reading his newspaper. The man who had taken their order brought the tall man coffee and a doughnut without exchanging words with him.

"Mama Jean wanted to know if you slept okay," Crab said, coming back to the booth. "I told her you slept most of the night. No use getting her all worried."

"She didn't say she wanted to talk to me?" Jimmy asked.

"I think she was fixing to go to work," Crab said. He twisted around in his seat and looked out the window. "What do you think of Cleveland?"

"It's okay," Jimmy said. He pictured Mama Jean getting ready to go to work. If it was cold she'd have her blue coat on, pulling it tight around her neck. She wouldn't wear gloves, no matter how cold it was.

A heavy girl brought their breakfasts, putting the plastic tubs of syrup for Jimmy's pancakes near his plate.

"I got some friends in Cleveland," Crab said. "We could stay here a while."

"I thought you had a job in Chicago," Jimmy said.

Crab pushed the bacon to one side and broke the yolks of his eggs with his toast. He blotted up the egg yolk with the toast and then put the toast in his mouth. "Yeah, I guess so," he said.

He looked tired.

The door opened and a man came in rolling a small barrel.

"Somebody go ask Paris if he wants some fish," the man said.

"He wants some fish," the girl who had served them said. "They fresh?"

"They so fresh they think they out for a walk on the beach," the man said, grinning and showing a gold tooth. "I told them I'm taking them back to the water soon as I have my coffee!"

"If they believe that then they some stupid fish," the man with the tools on his belt said.

"All fish are stupid," the fish man said. "That's why you can put them goldfish in a bowl and they just swim back and forth and don't even care."

"Give me twenty pounds of fish," the girl said. She had come around the counter and looked into the barrel. "They porgies, right?"

"Mostly porgies," the fish man said. "Got a few whitings in there, too."

"Yeah, well, make it thirty pounds," the girl said.

Jimmy saw Crab jump. He was holding back the curtain so he could see out the window. Jimmy looked over and saw a cop talking to the service station attendant. They talked for a while and then the cop walked on. Crab let the curtain go and went back to his eating.

By the time they had finished eating, Jimmy's

stomach was hurting again. Something was wrong. What he wanted to do, more than anything, was to talk to Mama Jean. He thought about asking Crab if he should, then thought better of it. He would just call when he had a chance.

"How much longer before we get where we going?" Jimmy asked as they walked across the street toward the car. A brown United Parcel Service truck stopped in front of them, and they waited until it moved on before continuing.

"You in a hurry?" Crab asked.

"Anything wrong with me wanting to know?" Jimmy came back.

"No, there's nothing wrong with you wanting to know," Crab said. "But I don't have forever to get a job."

"I'm thinking about calling Mama Jean," he said. The words surprised him, caught him unaware. On one hand he hadn't wanted to tell Crab, but in another way he did want to tell him to see what he would do.

"I think you want to get her upset," Crab said as they reached the car. "Get in."

"No, I'm going to call Mama Jean now." Jimmy looked around for a phone.

"Jimmy—" Crab started talking but Jimmy was already starting across the small island of the service station toward a pay phone he had spotted.

Jimmy reached the phone, took the receiver off the hook, started dialing, remembered he hadn't dialed the area code, and started dialing again. Crab's hand reached over his shoulder and pushed the cradle down, cutting him off.

Jimmy whirled around, his hands holding the

phone receiver in front of his chest.

"Why did you do that?" he said.

"Can I talk to you?" Crab asked.

"What you got to say?" Jimmy heard his voice rising.

"Just give me a little time, let me talk to you for ten minutes," Crab said. "All I'm asking is a chance, man."

"Go on, talk," Jimmy said.

"Let's get into the car, get on the road," Crab said.

"Why we can't talk right here?"

"Look." Crab turned around, saw the attendant looking at them, and turned back to Jimmy. "Jimmy, what I'm going to do, hurt you or something? I didn't come all the way to New York just to do something wrong to you. I just . . ."

Crab was breathing harder, his chest heaving. He looked at Jimmy and then away. There was something in his eyes, something at once frightening and sad.

"Why we can't talk here?" Jimmy repeated.

"Because the police are looking for me," Crab said.

Jimmy saw the attendant washing a car, but looking toward them. Down the street the policeman that had been talking to the attendant was talking to a postman. The postman's cart was between them.

Crab went back to the car and got in. Jimmy turned and walked in the opposite way. He didn't know what to do. He didn't know what to say to Crab. He didn't even know Crab.

There were tears in his eyes as he walked that broke up the light into tiny fragments. He thought about looking for a bus station, to get back to New York, but he wasn't sure why, or why he was afraid of Crab. But he was scared, scared and tired.

He stopped, turned back toward the service station. Crab had turned the car around and was pulling up alongside him.

"Look, just let me talk to you for a little bit," Crab said. "Then you can do anything you want to do. I can't make you do nothing anyway. Please."

Jimmy looked up the street, saw the attendant talking to the policeman, and got into the car.

Crab took the car through the downtown area of Cleveland. The streets were beginning to fill. As they got further downtown there were more people in suits than in work clothes. Jimmy sat as close to the door as he could get as Crab looked straight ahead. They made a left turn near a park and headed down a wide street. There were kids, white and black, on their way to school. They didn't look any different from the kids in New York.

Jimmy sniffled and was sorry that he did. He didn't want Crab to think that he was afraid of him.

They went into a park, drove along a lake, and then out the other side. Soon they were back on the highway again.

"I was up in Green Haven," Crab said. "I've been up there twice. The first time I was there it was for armed robbery. Then I was in jail in Rahway. Then I was back in Green Haven. I was in for eight years this time, and I was supposed to serve two more before I was eligible for parole. I don't think I was going to make no parole."

He took his right hand off the steering wheel and flexed his fingers. Then he took his left hand off the steering wheel and did the same thing.

"I wasn't feeling so good, you know, had this little thing and that little thing wrong with me. So one day I went up to the infirmary and told them I had pains in my back. They didn't say nothing about it, give me some aspirin. But the pains stayed. Turned out it wasn't nothing wrong with my back, but I was having kidney problems. They sent me to a hospital up there and the way they were talking . . ."

Crab looked away out the window. There were office buildings outside of Cleveland newer-looking than the ones in the city. Jimmy wondered how people could get to them to work. He looked over at Crab, trying to read his face, but couldn't.

"Then what happened?" he asked.

"Then what happened was I got to thinking," Crab said. "Sitting in my hole at night, couldn't half sleep, I got to thinking about you."

Jimmy looked away. "You didn't write."

"Yeah, I know. I wrote but I didn't mail you the letters because I never could get what I wanted to say down on paper."

"What did you want to say?" Jimmy asked.

"First I wanted to say that I loved you," Crab said. "Then that didn't sound right. You know, I figured maybe it wasn't even true. Maybe just because I found out I was really sick I wanted it to happen that way."

"What you got?"

"I don't know," Crab said. "They got a big word for it. Got to do with the kidneys mostly. They think they can save one kidney. Then I'd have to go on one of them machines that clean your blood out. But when they start operating on an inmate I don't know what they'd be thinking about. Maybe they would be serious, maybe not. I don't know."

"What does that have to do with Mama Jean?" Jimmy asked. "Why didn't you want me to call her?"

"You want her to get all upset?" Crab asked. "I thought you had more man in you than that."

Jimmy didn't answer.

"So I had to do for myself," Crab said.

"What's that mean?"

"I went to the hospital and I was pretty sick. I knew they're pretty relaxed in the hospital. One day last week they were cleaning my bathroom and the nurse let me go down the hall to use the staff bathroom. She got called away for something or the other and I went down the stairs."

"You mean you escaped from jail?" Jimmy asked. "Now the cops are after you?"

"Yeah, because . . ."

The sound that came out from Jimmy filled the car. He pounded the dashboard.

"Why don't you listen to me? Why don't you listen to me?" Crab grabbed Jimmy's clenched fist and pulled it from the dashboard. "I did it for you, Jimmy! I swear to God I did it for you!"

Jimmy felt himself crying, tried to hold it in, then just let it out. "You didn't do it for me, man!"

"Give me a minute! Let me tell you why I did it!"

"Stop the car. Let me out!"

Crab pulled the car over to the side of the road. He turned and grabbed Jimmy as Jimmy tried to get the door open. "I did it for you. Just let me tell you what happened. I'm just asking for five minutes of your time. I am your father."

"You ain't nothing!" Jimmy took a deep breath and tried to calm down. He wiped his face with his hands.

"I tried writing to you and nothing came out right. Nothing came out right and it made me feel like nothing. Just like you said. I ain't nothing and that's how I felt. I tried to think what you was going to say about me. What I said about my father. I used to say that my father couldn't give us much but at least I loved him. You can't say that. You don't even know me!"

"I know I don't love you!"

"That's okay! It hurts but it's okay," Crab said. "But I just wanted to settle one thing with you. That's the fact that I didn't kill those guards.

"No matter what else I done in this world I didn't kill nobody. I couldn't prove it to no judge, and the jury didn't believe me but I can prove it to you! I can prove it, Jimmy!"

Jimmy looked at Crab and saw that his eyes were red with tears.

"Why didn't you prove it . . . ?" His voice trailed off.

"Why didn't I prove it to the jury?" Crab gripped the steering wheel with both hands. "Because I didn't give them a reason to believe what I was saying, that's why. They knew I was a thief. They knew I didn't have an education. All they saw was another black man they had to pass judgment on. That's all. Why should they believe me?"

"Why did they say you did it in the first place if you didn't?"

"Can I tell you what happened on the day the thing went down?"

Jimmy shrugged. "If you want to."

"That's all I been wanting to do for the last year," Crab said.

He started the car again, checked his rearview mirror, and pulled back onto the highway.

"I was living up in the Bronx, on Daly Avenue. Some guys come over and said that they had a get over."

"A *what!*"

"A get over," Crab said again. "That's like something you can do to get some money or something. I was broke, and I didn't have a job."

"Where was I?"

"You were living with Jean; I figured she could take care of you better than me," Crab said.

"She said you sent some money sometimes," Jimmy said.

"She said that?"

"Yeah."

"Anyway, these two guys come over," Crab went on. "One guy was Richie Dutton, they called him Frank. The other guy was Rydell Depuis. Rydell didn't say much. Frank was doing all the talking. Frank was from Brooklyn but Rydell was a homeboy."

Jimmy tried to think what the men Crab was talking about looked like, but he couldn't think clearly. He kept asking himself why he was there. What had he done wrong to get God mad at him?

"What he said was there was this guy he knew worked at an armored car company," Crab went on. "This guy told him about this big shipment of money they were taking through a black neighborhood in Queens. He said when they stopped to pick it up they would stop at this delicatessen on Liberty Avenue and get sandwiches. We could hit them then."

"You mean stick them up?"

"Yeah. I told you I've done wrong; I'm not trying to hide anything from you. But I don't want you to think I killed anybody."

"Yeah." Jimmy looked out the window. There were large signs on the side of the road. He tried reading the signs backward to shut out the sound of Crab's voice. But he still heard him.

"So the thing was all set for that next Wednesday. I had a funny feeling about it. Anytime you mess with an armored car you taking a chance. The guards got guns, and you don't know if they're cowboy types or what.

"The day the thing was supposed to happen I woke up about two-thirty in the morning and the whole side of my head was busting open from an infected tooth I had. The whole thing was messed up. So when Frank and Rydell come over I told them I couldn't make it. I said maybe we could, you know, do the thing the next week. Rydell act like he was glad I had the toothache and he said okay. But Frank didn't want to hear it.

"We went back and forth a while and then they decided to go on and do it without me. That night I heard about it on the radio. On the radio it said that they thought it had been two Puerto Ricans had done it. They got away with something like three or four thousand dollars. It was just chump change. The radio said both of the guards had been shot and one was dead. I just thanked God I wasn't in on it."

"I thought you said that was what you was in jail for," Jimmy said.

"That's what they convicted me of," Crab said.
"That's not the way it was, though. The day after it
went down I went to the clinic and got my tooth
taken care of. When I got home three detectives
were waiting for me in the hallway. They didn't say
a word. They just started punching me in the stomach and throwing me around the hallway."

The car sputtered, stalled, and slowed down
quickly. The car behind them honked furiously as
it pulled around Crab. The car almost went off the
road before the engine caught again.

"Must be water in the tank!" Crab said. He shook
his head. "You okay?"

"Yeah."

Crab leaned forward, his arms draped around the
steering wheel, and took a deep breath as the engine
ran quietly. He looked at Jimmy, checked the rearview mirror, and pulled out into traffic again. This
time he stayed on the right-hand side of the road.

"So what happened then?" Jimmy asked.

"Then they took me up to my room — I was staying in a rooming house — and searched it and asked
me where I had hid the money. They asked me
what had happened to my face, and I told them I
just had my tooth pulled. When I told them that
they busted me all up in the face.

"They took me down to the precinct, and I was
in a lot of pain. A lot of pain, man. They took me
into a room and Frank was there. His head was
bandaged and his left arm was in a sling. They asked
him was I the one that was with him and he said
yes."

"Why he say that if you weren't there?" Jimmy
asked.

"I don't know." Crab shook his head. "The way
my lawyer figured it was that maybe he was the one
that did all the shooting. If he turned Rydell then
Rydell was going to point at him and say he did the
shooting. If he turned me I was going to say I was
innocent. Then he could cop a plea by saying I did
the shooting."

"What you say?"

"I told them the truth, just like I'm telling you,"
Crab said. "The jury didn't believe me. Once Frank
said he was in on the robbery they automatically
figured he was telling the truth about me. So everybody is happy. Frank got a light sentence, and the
cops got a 'solved' stamped on the case file. Whoever
the other guy was, I figured it had to be Rydell, got
away clean."

"If it was the truth they should have believed
you," Jimmy said.

"You believe me?" Crab asked.

Jimmy shrugged. Up ahead of them there was a
neon television with a real television picture on it
and a big sign beneath it that read SONY, THE AM-
ERICAN WAY.

"Do you believe me?" Crab asked again.

"I don't know," Jimmy said.

"You don't believe me," Crab said. "And you
don't have a thing in the world against me. And if
Frank was here saying it was me you really wouldn't
believe me."

"He still in jail?"

"He got eighteen months for testifying against me
and walked in ten. Then he got picked up for cutting
somebody to death and they got him in jail down
in Florida."

"How about the other guy?"

"Rydell? I don't even know if he was in on it or not because I didn't see him no more after that. I figured he must have been because he just disappeared. Anyway, I just found out where he lived about two months ago. Told you he's a homeboy. That's where we're headed, to my home in Arkansas. But I got to see some people in Chicago first."

"I thought you had a job in Chicago," Jimmy said.

"I might work there for a while," Crab said. "Till I get some cash."

Jimmy closed his eyes. He was getting a headache and his mouth felt dry. Every time Crab said something to him things changed.

"The guy you talking about" — Jimmy wished that he wasn't talking, but he couldn't help it — "he's going to tell the cops you didn't do it?"

"Rydell? I don't know. If he knows something that might help me, then maybe it'll be okay," Crab said. "But if he won't tell the cops nothing different maybe he'll tell you. That's the important thing."

They drove for four hours. Sometimes Crab talked, asking him things like what teams he liked or if he played ball.

Jimmy didn't know why he told Crab that he liked to play football. He hardly ever played football but sometimes he watched the team at the school work out.

After a while he found that his legs were tired. He was holding them tense. Even though he was riding in the car his whole body was tense. He tried to relax it but he couldn't.

They arrived in Chicago in the middle of the afternoon. Crab said he didn't hardly recognize it anymore.

"You've been here before?" Jimmy asked.

"Yeah, 'bout twenty years ago," Crab said. "Just after I got out of the army. I played with a little group here. Wasn't much of nothing, though. I was playing jazz, and they were playing blues. They could play up some blues but they weren't making any money."

"You know some people here?"

"Yeah. A girl I used to know from Newark moved out here a while ago. Got to see if she can help me get my hands on some money."

"How much you need?"

" 'Bout a thousand dollars," Crab said. "We don't want to bust into Arkansas looking like panhandlers."

They stopped at a bar, and Crab made several calls while Jimmy sat in one of the booths. Jimmy's mind flitted back to the highway, and his waking up to see Crab wasn't there. He thought about getting back to New York and wondered if the fifty dollars that Mama Jean had given him was enough.

"Mavis ain't up yet," Crab said, returning to the booth. "Her boy said she's got a night job."

"You got to get what you want at the bar," a light-skinned woman with full lips called over to Crab.

Crab went over to the bar and got a bottle of beer and a soda. While he was gone Jimmy felt for the money in the top of his sock. It was still there. He rubbed his leg and looked up at the ceiling as Crab came back to the booth.

"Got you a soda," Crab said. "You drink sodas?"

"Everybody drinks sodas," Jimmy answered.

"We're going to lay here for a while and then we'll go on over to Mavis's place."

"Okay."

"You hungry?"

"No," Jimmy lied.

"You know, you look a little like my brother," Crab said. He gestured toward Jimmy with the beer bottle. "Only you got those big eyes like your mama."

"You didn't know what I looked like before?" Jimmy asked.

Crab started to talk, or at least what sounded like words came out, but Jimmy couldn't understand them. Whatever it was it trailed off and Crab looked away.

There was a moment of silence between them, and then another one. Crab had his eyes open but didn't seem to be looking at anything.

"Sometimes I used to be talking about you," he said as if they had been talking all the while. "You

know, guys would be sitting around talking about
their kids. Mostly they talked about their boys because when you talk about your girls some of the
other guys start asking how she looked and getting
fresh. Right away that would get you mad. When
they talked about their kids I would talk about you
and then maybe I would think about you. I would
think what you could be like. If you were listening
to Jean, stuff like that."

"I don't give her any trouble," Jimmy said.

"Yeah, well, that's good," Crab said. He seemed
to be dozing off. "So what you got to say?"

"About what?"

Crab shrugged and got a faraway look in his eyes.

Jimmy thought he should say something. He
thought of asking Crab how it was in jail. That's
what he wanted to know. What did he do all day?
Then he thought talking about jail might get Crab
upset.

"What's your brother doing?"

"He got killed in Vietnam," Crab said. "He was
in the army about twelve, thirteen years when Vietnam broke out real good. It was always going on but
it wasn't broke out real good.

"He went through one pull over there and made
staff sergeant. They told him if he could make another pull he might even get to be an officer. He
made that first pull, then he made just about all the
second pull, eleven and a half months, and then he
got shot up. They brought him back to Texas, and
I went down there to see him. He wasn't no good.
He wasn't no bigger than you. He looked all eat up.
He died about two months after he got back from
Nam."

"You were sad?"

"What you figure?" Crab lifted the bottle of beer to his lips and tilted his head back. For a second Jimmy watched his Adam's apple bob. Then he looked away.

Crab spoke to the barmaid, got another beer and another soda for Jimmy, and wrote down something the barmaid was telling him.

He brought the soda and beer back to the table and went to the telephone and made a call. From the telephone he went to the bathroom. Jimmy touched the money in his sock again.

"We got us a place to stay tonight," Crab said when he had come from the bathroom. "A rooming house off State."

"Oh," Jimmy said.

They ate at McDonald's, and Jimmy saw that Crab had a roll of bills. He wondered if it was a thousand dollars.

They went to the rooming house first, and Crab paid a short white woman for a week's stay. The woman wore a wig that had slipped back on her head. There wasn't much hair on the front part of her head. The desk she sat behind was piled high with old magazines, and she had to clear a spot to count the money in.

She counted the money slowly, licking her thumb as she went through the sixty-eight dollars.

"You get clean linen now and on Saturday morning," she said, rubbing a stubby finger alongside her nose. "If you don't hand the linen back in you have to pay fourteen dollars."

The woman gave Crab the keys and leaned back from the desk.

"We'll pick up the linen when we get back," Crab
said.

They had parked the car down the street from the
rooming house near a construction site. When Crab
tried to start it again there was a whirring sound
and the car went dead. He tried it again and the
car's engine whirred again, this time at a higher
pitch as Crab pumped the accelerator pedal, then
coughed and stopped altogether.

Crab laughed. Jimmy had thought that he would
be angry, but he laughed instead. It was the first
time Jimmy had seen him smile.

"Car sounds like an old mule," he said. "It makes
a little noise but it don't move."

They left the car and took a cab to the house of
the woman that Crab knew.

The house was nice on the outside. It wasn't special, but it was a real house with a porch on the
front. On one side of the porch was a rusty bicycle
leaning against some old tires. On the other side
there was a card table. A radio on the card table
was between stations. There was music and a guy
giving the news at the same time. Jimmy thought
the woman who came out of the door and went to
the radio must have been the woman that they had
come to see.

"Now ain't you a sight for sore eyes," Crab said.

"Crab Little!" The woman came to the edge of
the steps and held out her arms. "Ain't you
something!"

"Ain't I, though?" Crab put his arms around her
and pulled her off the steps.

They started talking back and forth, almost at the
same time, and Jimmy stood to one side. He turned

his head when he saw Mavis's door open and a boy
that looked his age, maybe a year older, step out
and lean against the doorframe.

Mavis Stokes looked young, almost as young as
Cookie. A baseball cap sat at an angle from the side
of her head.

"How you doing? This your boy?" she asked Crab,
looking at Jimmy.

"Yeah, yeah. That's my boy."

"Well, he sure look like you," Mavis said. "Come
on in and sit down."

The boy stood at the door as Mavis and Crab went
in, but he never took his eyes from Jimmy. Jimmy
nodded as he passed into the house, but the boy
didn't acknowledge it.

"Frank, get Jimmy something to drink," Mavis
said.

They sat down, and Crab and Mavis started talking about somebody they had known a long time
ago named Tony. Mavis said Tony had bought five
cars and was now running a car service.

"Right here in Chicago?" Crab said.

"Right here," Mavis answered. "I mean, I never
thought that Tony would ever get into anything."

"Mmm-muh. Tony must have hit the number or
something."

"He didn't hit no number. He just went out and
saved his money."

Frank put some cans on the table, and Jimmy saw
that some of them were soda.

"You got a bathroom?"

"Right down the hall on the left, sugar," Mavis
said.

Jimmy went down the hall, pushed open the first

door he got to, and saw that it was the bathroom. He closed the door behind him, locked it, and checked the money in his sock again. He thought of Mama Jean and realized that he didn't even know how long he had been away from her. He had left in the evening. It was almost evening again. Two days. They were a long way from New York for only two days, he thought.

When he got out of the bathroom Crab was sitting at the table in the kitchen and Mavis was putting on her makeup in the mirror. There was a bottle of liquor on the table in front of Crab and he had a glass in his hand. The television was on and Jimmy sat on a chair in front of it.

"Frank's filling out nice," Crab said.

Jimmy looked over toward where Frank was placing rolls of tape on an end table.

"Since he been in that boxing thing he's been eating me out of house and home," Mavis said.

"It's good to be able to take care of yourself," Crab said. He poured himself another drink.

Mama Jean never drank. "I don't want to put nothing into this body I can't take out as easy as I put it in," she said.

"I got to go," Mavis said. "I just started this little piece of job so I'd better be on time. How long you guys going to stay in Chicago?"

"Depends on how things work out," Crab said. "Then we got to get on."

"Where you staying?"

"We got a place on Cahill, off State."

"You got a place already?" Mavis said. "I thought you just got here."

"Did," Crab said. "Had to find a place, though. Can't lay up on you."

Mavis looked over at Jimmy and smiled. "I would say something," she said. "But we got too many young ears in here."

"What kind of work you doing?" Crab asked.

"Working in a nursing home," Mavis said. "I'm off tomorrow. You and — what's your name, honey?"

"Jimmy."

"You coming over tomorrow for breakfast?"

"Yeah," Crab said. "And I'll bring over some Scotch."

"Talk that talk!" Mavis leaned over and kissed Crab. "Frank, don't you get hurt tonight at the gym."

"No problem," Frank said, smiling.

"And don't be staying out all night," Mavis said.

"And don't go over to Roosevelt," Frank added.

"They don't have nothing over to them projects but a whole lot of shooting and cutting," Mavis said. "And you better be over here tomorrow for breakfast, Crab."

"How long you been working nights?" Crab asked.

"For a while," she said, putting on her coat.

"Uh," Crab grunted. "You didn't write to me and tell me that."

"It ain't been that long," she said. "If I had knowed you was getting out then I would have written you and let you know. In fact, I would have come over and met you at the station."

"We drove to Chicago," Crab said. He looked at

Jimmy from the corner of his eye and then quickly away.

Crab and Mavis walked arm in arm to the bus stop. Frank had locked the door and followed Jimmy, carrying a gym bag.

Crab and Mavis kissed when the bus arrived.

"So where you going?" Crab asked Frank when the bus had pulled away.

"I got to go down to the gym," Frank said. "I got a fight coming up soon."

"How far's the gym?"

"About four blocks," Frank said.

"Yeah. You know, can we come watch you work out?"

"Sure," Frank said.

There was something about Frank that made Jimmy feel uneasy. Frank kept looking at him, sizing him up, letting him know that he was sizing him up.

"How old are you now?" Crab said as he looked down Martin Luther King Avenue.

"Sixteen," Frank said.

Jimmy felt glad that the boy was older than he was.

"I can make the Golden Gloves this year. My trainer said if I win two three-round fights he'll let me enter the Golden Gloves."

"You pretty good with your hands?" Crab asked.

"Yeah." Frank had a twisted smile. Jimmy thought that he was a nice-looking guy. Strong-looking. He had his hair cut close on the sides and a large letter *H* over a lightning bolt shaved into his hair.

The gym, although it looked small on the outside,

was large on the inside. The smell of sweat hung in the air. Fighters worked singly or in small groups. Some were shadowboxing, a couple were hitting punching bags, and some were just doing rope skipping or pushups.

Frank went into a dressing room, and Crab and Jimmy sat down on some wooden chairs in front of the ring. A little man came over to them. He was very, very dark and had very white hair.

"Y'all looking for something?"

"We're here with Frank," Crab said. "We're going to watch him work out."

"Unh-huh. Is he a young fighter, too?" he asked, looking at Jimmy.

Jimmy shook his head.

"Ain't got the heart for it, huh?" the old man said.

Jimmy shrugged.

"Maybe next year," Crab said.

Jimmy didn't look at Crab.

Frank came out and shadowboxed for a while. He didn't look that tough. Then he went to the small punching bag and began to hit it. He did that for about two minutes.

"That's to get your coordination together," Crab said.

"You know a lot about boxing?" Jimmy asked.

"Lot of guys boxed in the slam."

"The slam?"

"In prison."

"Oh." Jimmy had a vision of prisoners all dressed in black-and-white-striped prison suits and gloves boxing each other.

The old man who had spoken to Crab and Jimmy went over to Frank and turned back to Crab and

Jimmy. Jimmy wondered what he was saying. Frank nodded and got back into the ring. The old man called another boy over and pointed to the ring. The boy got in with Frank. They were going to box.

A couple of the other fighters came over and sat down near Jimmy and Crab. The old man blew a whistle, and the two fighters went to the middle of the ring. The boy who was against Frank was bigger than he was. He circled Frank, threw out both his hands, and pushed Frank back. Frank started jerking from side to side. He looked as if he knew what he was doing. Then he started swinging. He swung wild but he was hitting hard. He hit the boy up near his shoulders, and the boy started moving back.

"Side to side! Side to side! Don't back up!" the old man called out. "Keep your hands up!"

Frank came after the boy again. This time the boy didn't move back. He covered up and Frank flailed away at him.

"Don't just stand there! You got to fight back! You got to fight back!" the old man said.

The boy lifted his arm to swing at Frank. Frank hit him in the jaw. The boy fell down. The old man shook his head.

"He looking for a way to fall. I don't even know why he come to the gym."

"Some guys are like that," Crab said to Jimmy under his breath. "They just looking for a way to get out of a fight. They can lose. They don't care. Just as long as they ain't fighting, 'cause they don't got the heart for it. You know what I mean?"

Jimmy wanted to say that he did but nothing came out. He just nodded.

The boy in the ring got up shaking his head, and

the old man yelled at him. Told him he didn't have nothing in there to shake. Then they went on fighting. Frank went on beating the boy pretty bad. Jimmy wondered why the boy was in there if he didn't want to fight.

They fought the two rounds, and then the old man blew the whistle and said the fight was over. Then he called two more boys into the ring.

"You want to stay here. I got to go on downtown, see some people," Crab said.

"I'll go with you," Jimmy said.

"Yeah, okay. Let me tell Frank we going."

Crab walked over to where Frank was. Put his arm around him and said something to him. Frank nodded. Then he waved his fist at Jimmy and Jimmy waved his hand back.

On the way out Jimmy thought about how Crab had put his arm around Frank. He did it like they had something they knew, like they were friends or something. They had walked halfway down the block when Crab stopped.

"I forgot to ask him when Mavis gets home," he said. "Look, I got to make a phone call. Go on back and ask him when Mavis gets home."

Crab walked toward a phone, and Jimmy walked back to the gym. When he got in he looked around and looked for Frank. He saw him punching the heavy punching bag and walked over to him. The baggy gray pants Frank was wearing were dark with sweat in the back. When he saw Jimmy approach he moved closer to the bag. He pushed it with his head and bent his knees to get power into his punches.

Jimmy stood away from him, knowing that Frank

knew he was there. Frank grunted as he threw the punches, the sweat flying from his brow. He punched the bag hard, again and again, sometimes pushing it with his head, sometimes with his shoulder, so that it would swing into the proper position.

He doubled up on his punches, got wilder with his swings, and tried to punch the bag toward Jimmy. Jimmy saw that it wouldn't reach him and stood his ground. Finally Frank stopped the punching and, breathing heavily, looked over at Jimmy.

"Crab wants to know when Mavis gets home," Jimmy said.

"Why?" Frank asked. He hit the bag twice more, glancing blows that made it spin.

"He just told me to come ask you," Jimmy said.

"Where you from?"

"New York."

"New York? You think you bad, huh?"

"I didn't say I was bad," Jimmy said.

Frank hit the bag a couple of times. "I think you look like a punk. You look like a punk to me," he said.

"So you don't know when she gets home?" Jimmy said.

"I said I think you look like a punk," Frank said.

Jimmy turned and started walking away. Frank came after him. He could feel Frank coming. Frank grabbed him by his arm and spun him around.

"I didn't tell you to go, man," Frank said. "Look, I hit a man so hard once I broke his jaw. You know what I would do to somebody like you?"

Jimmy didn't say anything. He looked into Frank's eyes. That was the way you did it in New

York, he thought. No matter how scared you might be, you looked into their eyes.

Frank turned and walked away. "Tell him she'll be home at ten o'clock," he said over his shoulder.

Jimmy didn't turn back. He didn't know why Frank was mad. He knew that he didn't like Frank. He went out and saw Crab still talking on the telephone. He walked slowly up to the phone booth, regaining his composure as he did. Crab got off just as he reached the booth.

"What did he say?" Crab said.

"He said she'll be home at ten o'clock."

"Uh-huh. Come on, I got to go downtown. A friend of mine got me a job. I'll give you the address of the place we staying. You go on there and wait for me, okay?"

"I don't mind going on the job," Jimmy said.

"You go on to the place," Crab said. There was an edge in his voice.

"Yeah, okay."

"You think you can get to the place if I tell you how to go?" Crab asked. The edge was off his voice.

"I think so," Jimmy said. "I got to take a cab to it. Right?"

"You don't need no cab, man. I ain't got no cab money. Get the bus. Tell him you want to get off at Cahill Street. Okay?"

"Yeah."

Crab went through his pockets and found five dollars and gave it to Jimmy.

"I got to go on this job," Crab said. "You know, start getting some bread together."

"What kind of a job you got?"

"Gotta blow some horn, man," Crab said.

Crab gave Jimmy two dollars in change and pointed out the bus stop that Jimmy should take and watched as he went to it. When Jimmy turned back toward where he had left Crab, the older man was still standing in the same spot. Jimmy was crying. A man with a paper cup came up to him and asked if he had any "donations." Jimmy turned away as the man walked up to an older woman carrying shopping bags.

The tears were running down his face and, for the first time since he had met Crab, he was angry. He stood at the bus stop and looked at Crab down the street.

Crab started walking away from him, then began his stiff-legged run as he saw a bus coming. He got there in time for the bus and was gone first. Jimmy thought of looking around for a Greyhound station. He could start back to New York, he thought.

The bus came and Jimmy got on.

"I want to get off at Cahill Street," Jimmy said.

The bus driver ignored him.

On the way back to the rooming house Jimmy thought about how Crab sounded when he asked him about the job.

"Gotta blow some horn, man," he had said.

He said it like he was some kid in school being cool, or maybe like Frank, being tough. Sometimes he seemed okay, like a regular person. When he was acting like a regular person then Jimmy could think about what it would be like being around him. He could think about them driving and talking and looking at pictures. He hadn't even asked him about his mother. Not yet.

There were other things that he wanted to know,

too. He wanted to know what kinds of things Crab
had been thinking about in jail. Behind everything
was the moment in the hall when he had first heard
him speak. At the time Jimmy had been curious,
but he had been scared, too. Now the thought of
it, the thought of him and Crab in the hallway, was
like a shadow that darkened his memory, that filled
him with dread and wonder and delight. His father
had come from somewhere, from some place, from
some other time when his mother had been alive,
and when he had either been a baby or not yet born.
Nothing had gone wrong in his life then; it had been
a perfect time. He had simply been unaware of it.

"Yo, man, you want to buy a gold chain? Twenty-
four carat!" A dark hand held a chain in front of him.

"No," Jimmy said.

"You don't wear gold?"

Jimmy looked up into the face of a man who
looked young except for his eyes. The eyes looked
old, and Jimmy wondered if he was a crackhead.
"No," he said again.

The man looked at Jimmy and shook his head.

"I don't blame you," he said in a hoarse whisper.
"It ain't real. It's twenty-four carat and all but it
don't mean nothing in the real world. You know
what I mean?"

"Yeah," Jimmy said.

His mind drifted back to Crab. He started thinking about what Mavis had said. About how he and
Crab looked alike. He didn't think he looked much
like Crab, but Mavis had said that he did. But that
didn't mean a whole lot because a lot of people said
that he and Mama Jean looked a lot alike. Sister
Greene from the church always used to say, "Oh,

you sure can tell he's Jean's boy. Look how he favor
her."

Mama Jean said not to say anything to her. Just
let her think what she wants.

There was something else on his mind. He hadn't
wanted to think about it, but he did anyway. He
wanted to know if Crab liked him. The thought,
hidden away in the recesses of his own mind, still
embarrassed him, made him smile.

"You know why people wear gold?" The man sitting next to Jimmy spoke again.

"Why?" Jimmy asked.

"They're putting up a front," he said. He snorted
twice and looked away for a second and then back
at Jimmy. "I'm so messed around, a front don't do
me a bit of good."

Jimmy shrugged.

"I used to play some ball and stuff," the man said,
pointing with his thumb toward the back of the bus
as if he had played there, "but it got away."

"What got away?"

The man gestured with his hands, shrugged, and
drifted off to his own thoughts.

The bus lurched through the streets, picking up
passengers that never looked at each other. He saw
the man he had spoken to suddenly stand and reach
for the string that signaled the driver to stop the
bus.

"Almost missed my stop," he said, smiling. When
he stood Jimmy saw that he was a lot younger than
he'd first thought. "Be cool now."

Jimmy saw him look out of the door and then get
off the bus. Through the dark glass of the windows
he saw his head bobbing toward the sidewalk, and

then the man disappeared behind a truck.

He started thinking about Crab again. Crab had said that he had wanted to write to him and say that he loved him. That was a funny thing to say when he didn't even act as if he liked him. Crab could be so many different ways it was hard to figure him out. He was one way with Mama Jean, another way with Mavis, and another way with Frank. He seemed to like Frank. Maybe he thought that was the way Jimmy should be: tough, good with his hands. He had said he had boxed in prison.

"Cahill Street!" The bus driver shouted it out.

Jimmy thanked the bus driver and got off. It wasn't Cahill Street. It was already dark and he didn't see anything that looked familiar. He asked a lady if she knew where Cahill Street was and she pointed toward a wide street.

"Two blocks down," she said. "Walk down there and you can't miss it."

Jimmy found Cahill Street and looked at the key. "3B" was stamped into it.

The room was small and dirty. On one side a chest of drawers separated two single beds. On the other side there was a sink and small refrigerator. Two forks lay next to a two-burner stove on the sink counter. Jimmy looked for a bathroom, found it in the corner. It consisted of a tin-lined shower and a toilet with a broken seat. A roll of toilet tissue lay on the floor next to the toilet.

There was a pay telephone in the hallway and he thought about Mama Jean.

There were things to think about as he lay on the narrow bed. He wondered just how far he was from home. He had come to Chicago in a car. He didn't know how long it would take to get back to New York by bus. He was hungry, but it didn't make any difference. He would eat when he got back to New York. Mama Jean would have something on the stove, or she would go out and get something. Even if it was too late to get something, if the market was closed and the little bodega on the corner was closed she would still find something to eat. She always had. Mama Jean had been all that he thought he needed. Companion and friend, mother and father.

There were things to think about as he sat on the folding chair in front of the small table. He could have told Crab that he wasn't going with him. Mama Jean would have backed him up. The way Mama Jean looked at him, the way there was hurt in her eyes, he knew that's what she had wanted him to say. That's what he had wanted to say, too. Or at least a part of him had wanted to say it.

The room was dirty.

"There's not a reason in the world to live in dirt," Mama Jean would say, a bucket of hot soapy water in hand. "Not a reason in God's world."

An image of Crab playing a saxophone came into his mind. Just a few days before Crab had been in jail; now he was playing a saxophone in Chicago. Now he was watching Frank box, and talking to Mavis. Jimmy wondered if that was the way that things worked. You had things you did and they were always there for you to do.

"I'm your father," Crab had answered when Jimmy first saw him and asked who he was.

Maybe, Jimmy thought, being his father was just one of the things that Crab had to do.

Jimmy had always thought more about his mother than his father. It was easy to figure out what a mother was supposed to do. When he was young, when Mama Jean had sent him to St. Joseph's and the nuns had taught him about angels, he had thought of his mother as an angel. In his mind she was small with soft dark eyes, and she would look at him in a way that would make his chest fill up with feelings for her. Her face was small, too, and heart-shaped and when she smiled he could only see her two front teeth but they would be very white. Then he would think of her doing some of the things that Mama Jean told him that she did. Ice skating in the park or singing in the choir. They were good thoughts.

But sometimes, sometimes when he would wake

early in the morning, or when he was waiting to
cross a street far from home, he wondered about
the man he knew was in jail.

He hadn't wanted to be friends with him or anything like that. What he wanted most was just to
see him move. He wanted to see how he swung his
arms and maybe how he would wave when they met
on the street. He used to look at the picture in Mama
Jean's room.

"You want that picture?" Mama Jean had asked
him once when she caught him looking at it.

"What picture?" he had asked.

"You were looking at that picture of your daddy,"
she had said.

"No," he had said, not wanting to hurt her
feelings.

Still, when he got home from school the next day
the picture was on his bed. He didn't say anything,
just took it back to her room and threw it casually
on the dresser.

What he couldn't understand was how Crab had
just left him with Mama Jean in the first place.

He was hungry. Jimmy found the key and started
to leave, then remembered the fifty dollars in his
sock. He took it out and put it in the closet, wrapped
in his underwear, all the way to the back of the
closet.

The street was warm. There were some people
sitting on the stoop. A little girl leaned back and
looked at him through squinted eyes.

"You Chris's brother?" she asked.

"No," he said.

"You know he's not Chris's brother," someone
said.

Jimmy hadn't noticed the woman sitting in the first-floor window. When he looked at her she was drinking from a bottle of soda. She was the same woman who had given them the keys to the room.

He nodded a greeting, and she lifted her soda in return.

He walked down the street. There was a rib joint on the corner and a small grocery store just past that. He went in and saw a man sitting with a base-ball bat across his lap. A thin woman with her hair tied back was standing behind the counter reading the paper.

There wasn't much on the shelves, and Jimmy picked out a large bag of barbecue potato chips and a can of ginger ale.

"Dollar seventy-nine," the man with the baseball bat said.

Jimmy offered the man two dollars.

"Give it to her," the man grunted. "She behind the counter."

Jimmy gave the woman the two dollars and she took two dimes and a penny off the cash register drawer and pushed them across the counter.

"You want a bag, honey?"

"Yes."

The woman put the chips and soda in a bag and gave them to him with a smile. He smiled back at her. Then he looked at the man with the baseball bat.

"Don't be smiling at my woman, boy," the man said.

Jimmy smiled as he walked out.

The people in Chicago were friendly enough, maybe more friendly than in New York. He walked down the block. The streets were darker than New York. He could see down about four, maybe five blocks where there were more streetlights, but he didn't really want to go that far away. He walked another block. Mama Jean would have what she called a conniption fit if she knew he was going around the streets of Chicago alone. He hurried his steps back to the rooming house.

Once, when Eddie Grimes's father had come to school and hit Eddie right in front of the whole class, Jimmy thought of how he would feel if his father had come to school and hit him.

"Man, that was cold," Charles King was saying in the lunchroom.

Eddie said he felt like running away from home, but nobody believed him.

Jimmy had a whole scene he played out in his head. His father had come to school and got real mad when Mrs. Hodges said he didn't do his homework and stuff. Then his father had swung at him and hit him in the face. He fell down and his father was yelling at him. Mrs. Hodges was looking like she was happy and everything but then the expression on his father's face changed. He was looking at Jimmy funny.

In the scene Jimmy touched his face and saw that it was bleeding. He just walked away, knowing that his father was sad. But it was too late, he had already made Jimmy bleed.

"Hey, you Jimmy Little?"

If the woman's voice hadn't stopped him he would have passed the house.

"Yeah."

"You got a phone call," she said. "You got to call a number."

"You got the number?" Jimmy asked.

"Yeah, here it is." She gave him an envelope. He looked at it in the dim safety light next to the front door of the building.

It wasn't Mama Jean's number. He didn't recognize it at all. It had to be from Crab. The number was scrawled in big figures. Jimmy put the envelope in his pocket and walked into the building.

"You gonna call?" the girl called to him as he passed the office. "There's a phone in here."

She wanted to find out what the call was about. Jimmy nodded and went into the office. The girl opened the door a moment later and he went in.

"You got to dial nine first," she said.

It was like the phones in school, he thought. He dialed nine and then the number on the envelope.

In a way the phone call scared him. He didn't know why Crab would be calling him. Maybe he wasn't coming back or something.

"Hello?" Jimmy could hear music in the background.

"Yeah?"

"They told me to call this number?"

"Who told you to call this number?" the gravelly voice asked. "Who you?"

"I'm — is Crab there?"

"Yeah — just a minute."

Jimmy heard the phone hit something. There was still music in the background, and Jimmy figured it was a bar. Jimmy hoped he wasn't drinking a lot.

People who drank a lot or who took dope scared
him. They were like unreal people.

The woman who worked in the office looked
through a magazine. She looked over at Jimmy and
then up at the clock.

"They're getting him now," he said.

"You can't be staying on the phone too long," she
said.

"What's your name?"

"Doreen," she said. "That guy is your father?"

"Yeah."

"Where's your mother?"

"She died."

Doreen looked at him, shrugged, and went back
to her magazine, apparently satisfied.

"Hello?" The voice at the other end of the phone
seemed young.

"Hi," Jimmy said.

"Is this Jimmy?"

"Yes."

"My name is Billy Davis," the voice announced.
"I play horn over here at Vernon's. Your father is
sick, man. You got to come over here and get him."

"Where's Vernon's?"

"Emmett Street, down from the Loop."

"Where's the Loop?"

"You want me to find out where it is?" Doreen
looked up.

Jimmy handed her the phone.

Doreen got the address and hung up the phone.
She told Jimmy that he would have to get a cab and
that she would call him one if he had the money.

"I got it upstairs," he said. "I'll go get it."

"You finished with them potato chips?" she asked.

He handed her the potato chips and soda and went upstairs.

The ride to Vernon's took only ten minutes and came to four dollars and five cents. He gave the driver four dollars and fifty cents.

The dark man at the door put a big hand on Jimmy's chest. Jimmy started to tell him what had happened, and the man moved his hand and pointed. The sounds of a saxophone filled the room, pushing against the inverted pyramid of glasses on the bar, sliding along the sleek bodies posturing against the bar. Jimmy bumped into a body that turned out to be a man who ignored him completely. He couldn't see well at first. When he did see better it didn't help. There were wall-to-wall bodies.

He made his way down the dimly lit bar until he reached the end. He looked around and didn't see Crab or any other place to go.

Then there was a light and, for a moment, a silhouette appeared surrounded by a rectangle of light. The door closed and the man who came out, his horn hanging around his neck, lit up a cigarette.

"You Billy Davis?" Jimmy asked.

The man looked at Jimmy over his cupped hand. Then pointed to the door.

Jimmy knocked and the door opened. The first thing he saw when he walked in was Crab lying on the bed.

"You with Crab?" a fat man asked.

Jimmy nodded. Crab stirred and sat up, throwing his legs over the side of the couch he was lying on.

"I'm okay now," Crab said.

He stood and almost fell. The fat man grabbed his elbow. Crab turned and gave him a look and the fat man moved his hand away. For a moment the two men looked at each other. The fat man's look was steady. Crab's look was hard, really hard. Then Crab turned away and started toward the door.

"Got to get a cab," Crab said.

"You okay?"

"Yeah."

The crowd split for a moment, and Crab stopped to see the hatchet-sharp form of Billy Davis standing near the piano.

"That is the playingest sucker I ever heard in my life," Crab said. He said it quietly, almost reverently.

The sax seemed to spit out notes, throwing them helter-skelter across the tops of the sweating crowd. They came out with a fury, with abandon, stopping just short of rage. Then Billy Davis seemed to catch them, turning from side to side, swinging the sax as though he were rounding them up in a special order that only he knew. The sound was hard, and sweet, and clear enough to lighten up the darkness.

"He's good, huh?" Jimmy said.

"Yeah."

Crab started toward the door again. They bumped their way to the front door and out into the cool night air.

It had started to rain. Crab stood on the edge of the curb and flagged down the first two cabs he saw. Each pulled over and then sped away when they saw he was black. The third cab, driven by an old man, stopped.

"It's hard to find a cab on a rainy night like this," the old white man said. He looked nervously over his shoulder.

"Yeah," Jimmy said.

"He ain't going to get sick in my cab, is he?"

Crab was bent forward, his head between his knees. Jimmy started to put his arm around his shoulders, then stopped.

The two flights up the stairs took forever. Jimmy was aware of the sounds. Crab's feet against the tin-edged stair tread, the groan of the wooden banister as he pulled himself from step to step, the sound of his own breathing. He told himself that he wouldn't ask Crab if he was all right, he knew that he wasn't.

"You all right?"

"Give me your hand," Crab said. "No, let me put my hand on your shoulder."

Jimmy stood close to Crab, felt his breath against his cheek. There was the faint smell of liquor on Crab's breath. It wasn't that bad, and Crab didn't seem drunk.

"You want some water?" Jimmy asked.

"Yeah."

Jimmy looked for a glass, found one on the counter, and filled it with water. He started to bring it to Crab but realized it was probably warm. He opened the refrigerator to see if there was ice. The empty ice tray was on the top shelf. He brought the water to Crab and watched him bring it slowly to his mouth and sip it.

"What's wrong?" Jimmy asked.

"Back is tearing me up!" Crab said. "It's getting worse."

"You want me to get a doctor?"

"No, it ain't going to do any good," Crab said. "If I get some rest I'll be okay."

Jimmy sat on the other bed trying to think about what he should do. He looked at Crab, saw him trying to straighten out his legs and then wince. He pulled his legs back up and sucked in his breath slowly.

"You want more water?"

No answer. Jimmy sat back on the bed. He took off his shoes and put his feet up.

Crab tried to straighten out his legs again, got them further out, and stopped. He was breathing better, Jimmy thought.

"It feels better when I stretch out," Crab said.

"How does it feel when you don't stretch out?"

"It don't hurt all the time," Crab said. His eyes were closed. "Sometimes when I get too tired it starts up again."

"That's why you went to the hospital when you were in jail?"

"Something like that," Crab said. "Why don't you get some sleep."

Jimmy took off his pants and shirt and lay down on the bed. There was a light spread at the foot of the bed, and he pulled it over him.

"Good night," Jimmy said.

"Put the light out," Crab responded.

Jimmy listened for Crab's breathing in the darkness. He would breath once, a short little breath, and then a slightly longer one. Then there would be silence for a few seconds until he breathed again.

Jimmy said a quick prayer. He hoped that Crab would be all right. He wouldn't even think about him dying. He wouldn't think about it and that was all he could think about. It was like a shadow that fell over him in the darkness.

"What we going to do tomorrow?" Jimmy said softly, almost to himself.

"Get Mavis and Frank and start off to Arkansas," Crab said.

"You got the money?"

"No, but I don't have the time to waste in Chicago, either," Crab said.

"You play the horn?"

"Hoped I'd have a chance to play. I played a lot up in the slam. Mostly every day when I had a reed. Sometimes you mess up your reed, or the guards come and just mess them up, put chips in them, stuff like that. Then you can't play."

"They didn't let you play?"

"No, they let me play," Crab said. "They had to let me play. I played with Vernon before. He fronts the place. He said some Polish guys from Milwaukee own it but he fronts it pretty good. I used to play with him and you saw that Billy Davis."

"I saw him playing," Jimmy said.

"I taught him how to play that horn. He used to come around to the club and just stare at everybody. I had this old piece of horn I won in a blackjack game. I told your mama about him, and she told me to give him that piece of horn."

"My mother was here in Chicago?"

"She wasn't your mother then. We were just going together. I brought her out here to Chicago just to see what it looked like."

"She saw Billy Davis, too?"

"He wasn't nothing much to see, then." Crab's voice seemed to relax. "I showed him some, Vernon showed him a little, and the rest he just picked up on his own."

"You played with him tonight?"

"I can't play with him," Crab said. "I can't play with none of these guys. I busted in and ran my mouth and talked like I was doing something. Then I asked him to let me gig for a couple of days so I can pile up some stash. He said he'd have to hear me play after the first set.

"I went out and listened to one group and they were smoking. Then Billy and his little trio came on and they just did the whole thing. Listening to that boy playing I knew I couldn't do nothing that came even close. Guy said he'd let me use his horn, and I couldn't even put my hand out to reach for it. Anything I could have been is gone. Got myself all aggravated. That's why my back started acting up."

"So how you going to get the money to get to Arkansas?"

"We just got to get there," Crab said. "Just got to find a way."

"How far is Arkansas?" Jimmy asked.

Crab didn't answer.

Jimmy lay in the darkness. He was afraid for Crab. He had seen him in pain and heard the disappointment in his voice. He wondered if Crab felt the same way that he had when he had seen Frank hitting the bag.

When Crab was like this, hurt and feeling bad, it was easier to be with him, Jimmy thought.

Jimmy was up first and went out and got a container of coffee and some doughnuts, the way he had done a lot of times for Mama Jean. When he got back Crab was shaving. He had a towel wrapped around his side, and Jimmy saw that he was thinner than he had thought at first.

"How you doing?" Jimmy asked.

"Okay."

"I got coffee and stuff."

Crab finished shaving and went into the shower.

Jimmy ate one of the doughnuts. He had used the money he got from Mama Jean to buy them. He thought again about going back to Mama Jean, but in his heart he knew he was going to Arkansas with Crab.

Crab finished his shower and came out drying himself. Jimmy looked the other way. He was aware of Crab taking the coffee.

Doreen was sitting in the office by the time they got downstairs. Jimmy imagined her sitting there all night with her eyes closed, opening them suddenly when the first people came down in the morning. Crab called Mavis from the corner. He was different than he had been the night before, livelier, his eyes wider open.

When Mama Jean wasn't feeling well, or when she was tired, she walked as if her feet were heavy. Sometimes she would seem to drag them along, shifting from side to side to get them going. When she was feeling well she would walk with her head thrown back and her feet moving straight ahead.

When Crab was feeling good he walked with his chin down and his legs stiff, as if he were walking against a strong wind.

"She's going to meet us on LaSalle Street at eleven," Crab said. "It's nine-thirty now. By the

time we get down there it'll be ten. We got to wait
for a while. Maybe we can get some breakfast or
something."

"Okay." Jimmy shrugged.

Crab wasn't asking him anything, he was telling
him. It was okay, he thought, for Crab to tell him
what to do. But it was different. Mama Jean never
told him what to do. In a way she told him, but it
was different the way she did it. Mama Jean would
tell him to do things, but the way she would tell
him, putting her hand on his arm or rubbing his
shoulder, it was almost as if she were asking him.

They took the overhead train and got to their stop
at five minutes to ten. There was a coffee shop at
the corner where they were supposed to meet Mavis
and they sat in it. They could see the corner in case
she showed up early. Crab ordered eggs over easy
and ham, and Jimmy asked for cereal.

"We rent a car and we can get down to Arkansas
in about fourteen, fifteen hours," Crab said. "Soon
as we hit Arkansas we got to watch our speed. They
grab you in a minute for speeding down there."

"How come Mavis is going with us?"

"She's my lady," Crab said. "Haven't you got a
lady?"

Jimmy looked at Crab and saw him smiling. "I
don't have a lady," Jimmy said.

"Plenty of time, plenty of time," Crab said.
"When I was your age my daddy had two ladies.
He had my mama at home and then he had this
little girl cross town. I was never interested in a
whole lot of women. All they do is get you messed
around."

"How about Frank?" Jimmy asked. "He going, too?"

"Yeah."

The waitress brought their breakfasts, placing a large plate of toast between them.

"The toast got margarine or butter?" Crab asked.

"Margarine," the waitress said, turning to go away.

"Take it back!" Crab said. "Bring me some butter."

The waitress sucked her teeth and took away the toast.

"Is Frank your kid, too?" Jimmy asked.

"Naw," Crab said. "He's Mavis's kid. Why do you ask?"

"Just asked," Jimmy said.

"You like him?"

"No." Jimmy poured milk on his cereal. "He was messing with me the other day when I went back into the gym. Called me a punk and stuff."

"Somebody call you a punk you got to stand up to them," Crab said. He paused while the waitress put a new plate of toast on the table. "People figure you either got heart or you a punk," he went on. "If you stand up to them then they figure you got heart and they don't try to dis you."

"Why he try to dis me when he don't even know me?" Jimmy asked. "I didn't say anything to him."

"Some people are just like that," Crab said. "You got to learn what people are like."

They finished their breakfasts and Crab ordered more coffee.

Jimmy thought that maybe Frank was right.

Maybe he was a punk. He hadn't wanted to stand up to him.

"Suppose I dis Frank back, and we get into a fight," Jimmy said. "You think I can beat him?"

"You know anything about fighting?" Crab asked.

"No."

"Then how you going to beat him?"

Jimmy turned to look through the plate glass window. On the street a few people had umbrellas up. A nun held out her hand, palm up, and looked toward the heavens. There were two women crossing the street. Both of them were laughing and both of them were wearing baseball caps. There was also a man waiting at the bus stop wearing a baseball cap. Jimmy wondered if more people wore baseball caps in Chicago than in New York. He wondered why Crab thought he should stand up to Frank if he didn't think he could beat him.

"If I got some time I'll teach you about fighting," Crab said. "All you got to know is that you ain't in no dancing match. Most of the people think they fighting when all they want to do is to dance around. A fight's a fight. You got to want to hurt somebody before they hurt you."

"That's what you want to do?" Jimmy asked. "Teach me to fight and things?"

"You want to learn?"

"Yeah," Jimmy said, figuring that was what Crab wanted to hear.

"I got some things to do," Crab said. "But if I got some time I'll teach you how to fight."

"Okay."

Jimmy looked out to the street again. He could

see the rain falling now. It was harder than it was
before, but still not that bad.

By the time they left the restaurant it was ten
past eleven. They stood under the marquee of a
building close to the door to stay out of the rain.
Once in a while Crab moved to the side of the door
and leaned against the building. By eleven-thirty
Jimmy saw that he was upset. The lower part of his
jaw tightened and loosened.

"They're late," Jimmy said.

Crab looked away down the street without saying
anything. There was an old-fashioned-looking clock
over a clothing store across the street, and Jimmy
tried to see if he could see the minute hand moving.

Crab gave Jimmy a five-dollar bill and told him
to go into the drug store and buy some aspirin.

"You gonna be okay?"

"Yeah."

The drugstore was crowded. On one side there
were magazines, and on the other side there was
liquor. He went to a young man in a gray coat and
asked him where they kept the aspirins. The clerk
pointed toward some stairs that led to a lower floor.

Jimmy went down and found the aspirins. There
were at least five kinds and Jimmy picked one that
he had seen on television. He paid for them with
the five-dollar bill, counted the change out carefully,
and made sure he had the receipt.

When he got upstairs it was raining harder and
there was a small knot of people around the front
door. Jimmy put the aspirins into his pocket and
pushed his way to the door.

He didn't see Crab. For a moment his heart was

beating faster, then he tried to calm himself and walk to the building they had been standing in front of before. He thought that maybe he had made a mistake, but the clock across the street was still there and he knew he hadn't. It was a little after twelve.

He shivered and pulled his collar closed against the gusting wind.

He thought, if Crab didn't come back, he could call Mama Jean collect and she would find a way for him to get back to New York. He moved back closer to the building as the wind picked up and sent the rain under the marquee. He was surprised that he was worried about being left alone in Chicago. He had never been afraid in New York. That was what his life was like. It was different now than it had been. He wondered if it was more like what Crab's had been. He told himself that no matter what happened, even if Crab did leave and he couldn't call Mama Jean collect he wouldn't steal anything.

"Come on!" Crab went by him quickly.

Jimmy, surprised, started after him. Crab walked on, mindless of the rain or the crowd. People moved out of his way. They walked two blocks and then Crab turned into a hotel.

The doorman looked them over as they walked into the lobby. Crab walked over to a black guy in a uniform and asked him where the bathroom was. Jimmy noticed that Crab had pressed a bill into the guy's hand.

"Go past the elevators and turn left."

In the bathroom Crab used the urinal and then

washed his hands. He combed his hair and looked at himself in the mirror.

"How do I look?" he asked Jimmy.

"Okay."

"Come on." Crab went out into the lobby of the hotel and looked around. Then he went over to a counter near the newsstand. It was a car rental office.

The young girl behind the counter was pretty. She smiled at Crab and asked him what he wanted. He told her he wanted a Ford.

"Something mid-sized," he said.

She gave him some papers to fill out. He started filling them out. Jimmy watched him. He saw him put down "Robert Daniels" in the name spot.

"Go sit down." He pointed toward the seats near the piano.

Jimmy sat down and looked at his knees. He didn't know what Crab was doing, but he was pretty sure it was wrong.

The renting didn't take too long. Jimmy looked up long enough to see Crab give the girl a credit card. She made a phone call, then handed it back to Crab. Then he got the keys and called Jimmy over.

They stopped at the newsstand and Crab bought some cookies and two sodas. Then they went around the corner and showed the keys to an attendant in the parking lot. The attendant took the keys and went away.

Jimmy didn't say anything, even when Crab asked him for the aspirins. He just took them out of his pocket and gave them to him.

When the car came Crab gave the attendant a dollar. He got into the driver's side and pushed the passenger door open for Jimmy. When Jimmy was in they pulled out of the lot and down the street.

Crab drove slowly through the crowded Chicago streets until he got to a bridge. Then he pulled off to one side of the road, opened the aspirins, and took them with some soda.

"Where's Mavis and Frank?" Jimmy asked.

"They're not coming," Crab said. He closed the aspirins and reached across Jimmy to put them into the glove compartment.

"How come?"

"Why should they come to Arkansas?" Crab asked. He looked into the side mirror and then pulled back onto the highway.

"You said they were coming," Jimmy said. "I thought they were coming."

Crab took a drink from the can of soda, turning his head sideways so he could still see the road. He put the soda down and clutched the steering wheel with both hands. Jimmy turned and looked behind them. Chicago had some tall buildings, he thought.

The rain picked up again, coming in the windows.

"Roll up your window," Crab said.

Jimmy looked for a way to roll up the windows and couldn't find anything. He looked at Crab and saw him looking, too.

"We gonna drown in the car," Jimmy said.

Crab looked at him and smiled.

It was a warm smile. The best smile he had ever seen from Crab, and it made him feel good. He tried to think of something else that was funny, but couldn't. Maybe it was better if he didn't say anything. Just leave the smile where it was, nice. Warm. Friendly.

Crab found the buttons for the windows and put them up. Then he found the wiper button. He pushed it and the car swerved violently.

Crab hit the wiper button again but the car still swerved. He held the wheel with both hands and braked quickly. The rear end of the car slid toward the middle of the road, and Jimmy caught himself before he slammed into the dashboard. The car came to a skidding stop on the shoulder.

"Man, what happened?" Crab hit the wiper button again and the wipers went on obediently. He turned them off and tried to straighten the car out. There was a flopping sound.

"What's the matter?" Jimmy asked.

"You hurt yourself?"

"No," Jimmy lied, ignoring the pain in his cheek where his face had met the dashboard.

Crab got out and looked at the front of the car. Then he came and took the keys from the ignition.

"Flat tire," he said. "Probably happened just as I turned on the wipers."

He went to the back of the car and took out the spare tire. When Jimmy saw the tire he got out. The rain was still coming down, harder than it had been before.

Crab put the jack under the car and jacked it up. He went back to the trunk to look for more tools but didn't find any. Then he looked at the jack handle and saw that he could use that to get the hubcap off. He got the hubcap off and used the same tool to start taking off the wheel.

"You know why I'm here?" he said. The rain was mixing with the sweat on his face.

" 'Cause Mavis and Frank don't want to go to Arkansas?" Jimmy asked.

"No, I mean why I walked away from the slam?" Crab said. He had taken off his jacket and was kneeling on it. "Put this nut in the hubcap."

"You said you wanted to go to Arkansas," Jimmy said.

"Yeah, because I knew I was fooling myself," Crab said. "I was in the slam thinking maybe I was going to get better, then serve my time and start all over. Then one day a friend of mine died."

"In the place?"

"Yeah, when you're outside you don't think about people dying in jail. You think about them serving their time and getting out. But a lot of cats kick off in the slam. Some of them get wasted by other inmates. Some of them get sick, like me. Then some of them just get sick of living. You know what I mean? They just get sick of the whole thing. Life doesn't have any meaning they understand so they try something else. And the only thing they know other than living is dying."

Crab took off the last nut and handed it to Jimmy. He was breathing hard.

The spare was lying on the side of the road, and Crab got it and tried to fit it on to the wheel. It didn't go on, and he slammed it down to the ground.

"What's the matter?" Jimmy asked.

"It don't fit. They got the wrong tire in the trunk."

"Can you get the car up higher?"

Crab looked at him, then picked up the tire again and put it against the wheel. He saw that he hadn't jacked it up high enough the first time, put it down, and jacked the car up higher. He tried the wheel again and it fit. He put it on and started replacing the nuts.

"I figured that I was fooling myself in the slam," Crab said. "All my life I was just jumping back and forth. One day I'm saying that I'll get out and start all over again. Then the next day I'm saying that I'm going to do something to get rich. And when I get out I find that I'm still Crab, and this is still the same old world. You know what I mean?"

"Sort of," Jimmy said.

"I figured all I had was a kid someplace. A kid that hated me because I killed somebody."

"I don't hate you," Jimmy said.

The tire was on, and Crab lowered the car. "Put the old tire in the trunk," he said. Jimmy put the tire in the trunk and then picked up the jack and the tool and put that in the trunk, too. The tire was heavier than he thought it would be.

Crab got the hubcap on after a few kicks and got back in the car. Jimmy was cold and wet when he got in.

"You got the keys?" Crab looked at Jimmy.

"No."

Crab got out and looked at the ground where he had been kneeling, then went to the back and found the keys in the trunk. In a minute they were on their way.

"When I got out and started moving around I forgot what I knew. Started figuring like I used to before I got into trouble. Thought I could play the horn 'cause I fooled around with it inside. Thought I could come out and hook up with Mavis again."

"Maybe they were just late," Jimmy said.

"I called her. Said she had other things to be doing. Asked me who I thought I was."

"She said that?"

"Yeah, she's right, too."

"I had it figured right in the slam, then I got in

the air and forgot everything. All I got in this life is
you. And I don't even know you."

"I don't hate you," Jimmy repeated.

"It's not that simple," Crab said. "That doesn't
fill anybody's need."

"What do you need?"

Crab reached down to the side of the seat and
felt around until he found the lever that adjusted
his seat.

"I guess I need something good to think about
myself," Crab said. "I need to look in a mirror and
see something I can respect. Maybe even look at
you and see something I can respect, and that re-
spects me."

Jimmy didn't answer. He didn't know what Crab
wanted to think about, or how he was going to make
it come out right. He didn't know what he was supposed to say to Crab, either.

He looked down at the seat and saw that there
were only a few inches between them. It was a few
inches and yet it was a long way.

"Why you put down that other name at the car
place?" Jimmy asked.

" 'Cause I'm sick to dying, man," Crab said, looking straight ahead. "It don't matter how I get what
I need."

The miles hissed by. They were out of the rain
but the sky was still a cold, humorless gray. Crab
sighed a lot, lifting his shoulders up and forward,
exhaling the breath with a loud huffing sound. Then
he would move his rear end in the seat as if he were
looking for a right way to sit.

The miles hissed beneath them as the houses and

billboards and gas stations blurred in their vision. Jimmy searched for words. There was something he felt, something that Crab had almost said.

Jimmy thought of some things to say, things like "I like you," but they didn't work. He didn't really like Crab. He wanted to know about him, he almost had to know about him, but he didn't really like him. But he thought that one day, if things worked out, he could.

"What was your father like?" Jimmy asked.

"C. C. Little?" Crab smiled.

"That was his name?" Jimmy asked. " 'C. C.'?"

"Yeah, that was his name. Or at least that's what everybody called him." They were passing a Greyhound bus and a small boy waved from the window. Jimmy wanted to wave back, but didn't want Crab to see him do it. "I used to see him about twice a month. He was a cook on the Southern route. His real name was Charlie — maybe even Charles. But they used to call him C. C. for County Circuit. That's like in that song — 'C .C. Rider.' You know that song?"

"No."

"Probably before your time," Crab said. "Anyway, he would cook on that route. They used to cook good food on trains, you know. He'd be gone for weeks at a time. Then when he did get off the road he would cat around until he had to come home to get his clothes clean. He'd come on home and my mama would wash and iron his clothes and then he'd be gone. Sometimes he'd bring some sugarcane home if he went down to Louisiana. The train used to go into New Orleans. It didn't go into Texas in those days."

"You used to hang out with him?"

"My daddy?" Crab shook his head. "He was busy on the train, then he had his friends. He didn't have much time for children."

"Why?"

"That's just the way his life went," Crab said.

"He lived with you?"

"Yeah, when he was home."

"He lived with you and he never hung out with you?"

"One time, I was twelve. I know I was twelve because I had a rifle that I got for my twelfth birthday," Crab said. "Anyway, he was going hunting and my mama told him to take me. He didn't want to take me, but when it was time to go he told me to get in the back and keep my mouth shut. They were hunting 'coons.

"It was early morning when we went out. We went around in the woods for a while. There were five men, including my daddy, and me. The dogs we had weren't much and neither was the guys hunting. We ran around the woods for most of the day. I think they killed some birds and a couple of hares. Then they went to an old shack one of them had out in the woods and they built a fire and sat around the fire and drank for the rest of the day. My daddy offered me a drink and I told him I didn't want one.

" 'You in the company of men, now,' he said to me. 'You got to act like a man acts.' And I took a drink, and I felt pretty good."

"You hang out much after that?" Jimmy asked.

"That was the only time he ever took me with him," Crab said. "I was in jail when he died."

"That make you feel sad?"

"Didn't make me feel sad. Didn't make me feel nothing, really." Crab shook the soda can and found it empty. Jimmy gave him what was left in his. "Hand me that aspirin out of the glove compartment."

Jimmy handed Crab the aspirin and watched him open the small bottle with one hand, flipping the top off with his thumb and making it sail against the windshield. It bounced near Jimmy and then onto the floor of the car. Jimmy picked it up and handed it to Crab.

"If he didn't like you, who did he like?" Jimmy asked.

"He liked women, mostly," Crab said.

"Like Mavis?"

Crab turned and looked at Jimmy. He shook his head and lifted and dropped his shoulders twice. "I don't like Mavis," he said. "Not that much. Messing with Mavis means that I'm into life. You know what I mean?"

"No."

"Means I'm doing something. I got a woman, I got something to do with her."

"Did you like your father?" Jimmy asked.

Crab turned on the car radio, pushed buttons until he found a station he liked, and pulled off into the fast lane.

Jimmy wanted to ask Crab how his father had looked. He tried to imagine Crab as a boy, sitting next to his father. It was a hard thing to do, imagining an adult as a child. Looking at Crab in the car, as the day waned and the neon lights flashed against the sharp angles of his face, it was hard to imagine him as anything but what he was, a strange, dark man hunched over the wheel of a rented car.

After a while he felt himself going to sleep and gave in to it. He thought of Mama Jean, an impossible distance behind him. In front of him, somewhere in the darkness, lay Arkansas.

When Jimmy woke, the dawn was just breaking between two white buildings. The car was parked on a small street under a tree. His heart jumped when he saw that Crab wasn't next to him. He looked in the backseat and saw Crab asleep, curled up so that he looked smaller than he was.

The sky was mostly gray but a streak of white stretched itself from the end of a flagpole. It was hot in the car, nearly suffocating. The windows were closed. Jimmy pushed the buttons that raised and lowered the windows, but nothing happened. He checked Crab again, listened for a moment to his low raspy breathing, then opened the door. There was a breeze, not much, but it was something. It cooled his brow with its freshness. There was a smell he didn't recognize. The sky was already lighter than it had been when he first awakened — the white streak had broadened into a patch of brilliant day.

He stood up, stretched, and noticed that he had to go to the bathroom. The street was deserted.

There were mostly trucks parked along one side of the street; the other side was empty. There was a wrought-iron fence still in shadow, and Jimmy walked over to it, looked around, and relieved himself.

He got back into the car and closed the door quietly. He looked back at Crab. He could hardly distinguish his features in the dim light.

A truck rounded the corner and moved down the street toward the car. Jimmy sunk down beneath the dashboard, listening to the hum of the truck's motor as it neared, then passed him.

He looked up to see the truck continue down the street. He wondered how long they had been parked. Maybe Crab had just gone to sleep in the back, he thought, or maybe he had been asleep a long time and wanted to get up early. He looked at the clock in the car. It was five fifty-three. A car came down the street, stopped in front of the lighter of the two buildings he saw, and a dark figure got out and went to the front of the building. A moment later whoever it was that had gone to the front door had gone in and the car pulled away from the sidewalk. Jimmy looked at the clock again and saw that it was five fifty-four. Jimmy thought that people would be just coming to work.

"You awake?" he asked. He put his hand on Crab's shoulder.

Crab grunted. Jimmy put his hand on Crab's shoulder again. This time he just left it there.

It was funny touching Crab. He had talked to him, had shook his hand, but he hadn't really touched his body before.

"Crab?" He spoke softly. He pushed his fingers

gently into the shoulder that hunched forward in the semidarkness. The shoulder was hard, and Jimmy didn't know if it was muscle or just bone. He felt his own shoulder. Soft. Not really soft, but softer than Crab's.

"Hey, you awake?"

Crab stirred and opened his eyes. "What time is it?" he said, his voice barely audible.

Jimmy checked the car clock again before answering. "Six oh seven," he said.

Crab exhaled heavily, then put his hand on the headrest of the back of the front seat and pulled himself upright. "You know you snore when you sleep?" Crab asked.

"No, I don't," Jimmy said.

"Yes, you do," Crab said. "Got you a little baby snore. When your mama first brought you home from the hospital you used to snore. She thought it was the cutest thing."

"What did you think?"

Crab turned and looked out of the window. The morning light broke his face up, giving him a shine on the lower part of his face that made him look scared. He shrugged, as if he were answering a question he had asked himself. Then he pulled his legs out straight, first one and then the other. He rubbed them both, then opened the car door and got out.

"We in Arkansas?"

"Just about there," Crab said, leaning against the car, his elbow in the car window. "We're in Memphis, Tennessee. We go cross the river and we in West Memphis. That's in Arkansas. Then we go on down the road a bit and we're in Marion. That's my home."

Crab took a step and then grunted. Jimmy looked over the back of the seat. Crab was standing against the car so that his chest was at the window. Jimmy thought he was all right, then he saw his left hand holding onto the door frame. The fingers were tight, the calloused knuckles seemed to tighten and relax. Crab grunted again.

Jimmy got out of the passenger side of the car and looked over at Crab. Crab had his forehead down on the blue-silver top of the car.

"You okay?" he asked.

No answer. Crab's head was still down on the top of the car.

"You want me to get the aspirins?" Jimmy asked.

Crab straightened and moved his shoulders up and down to relax them. Then he started walking toward the back of the car. Jimmy walked around to the back.

"I can walk it out," Crab said.

He walked around the car, holding on with one hand, his feet shuffling forward. There were small beads of sweat on his forehead. Jimmy moved out of his way and leaned against the car. He thought about getting back in, but he wanted to be outside in case Crab fell.

Crab walked for almost five minutes before he got back into the car. Jimmy got in with him. Crab didn't say anything, just pointed to the glove compartment.

Jimmy gave him the aspirins.

"It hurts bad, huh?"

"Yes." Crab started the motor. "When I sit still a long time. I got to either walk around or stay with a heating pad under my back."

"You been to a doctor?"

"Didn't you ask that question before?"

"What did you say?"

Crab turned halfway round in the seat to look down the street, then pulled away from the curb. "Doctor can't do me no good," Crab said. "All I got to do now is to get my stuff together."

"What stuff?" Jimmy asked. He turned away from Crab as they passed a small house. There were three cats, two black and one gray, sitting on the porch railing and a thin woman, her white arms coming from strange angles in the faded flower jumper, standing in the doorway behind them.

"I got to make Rydell tell the truth," Crab said.

"If he tells the truth are they going to let you out of jail?"

"By the time they get around to fixing up the paper work . . ." Crab's voice trailed off. "You hungry?"

"No," Jimmy lied.

They drove for another five minutes before Crab pulled over and asked a stoop-shouldered man which way the bridge was.

"You mean the 'M' bridge?" the old man asked.

"Yes." Crab nodded his head as he spoke.

"Go down this street until you get to the second light." The old man spat on the ground. "Then you make a left and go down the street until you see Carroll's. You get to Carroll's and look over past the filling station and you can't miss it."

" 'Preciate it," Crab said.

They went down one block and saw signs that led to the bridge.

"We get over to Marion you got to be careful about what you say," Crab said. "Rydell knows where I've been, but he doesn't know I walked out."

"Okay."

Jimmy looked at the clock in the dashboard. It read "8:24." Memphis, Tennessee, was just waking up. The cars that made their way through the early morning streets were old, many of them covered with dust. Workers, many of them in overalls, walked with measured paces down the streets. In the filling station they were to look for there were three pickup trucks parked near a vending machine, and overweight men drank coffee out of blue containers.

They reached the bridge, with Crab stopping while a dog finished investigating a paper bag in the roadway. Two boys leaned against the fence next to the bridge to watch.

"That's Memphis for you," Crab said. "Some places it's as busy as New York, but in the background it's more relaxed. People stop to watch the world go round."

Where Memphis, Tennessee, was just waking, West Memphis seemed still asleep. They passed houses that all seemed to be leaning away from the road. The porches in the first part of town were high, with slats missing from the latticework and small flowerpots that seemed always out of place.

"Look at that." Jimmy pointed to the dark smoke pouring out from the chimney of one of the houses.

"Coal stove," Crab said. "That dirty smoke got to be coal. Wood burns clean. Sometimes people go

down to the yards and steal that soft coal. Stuff burns
terrible."

As they went through the town the spacing between the houses increased until the town seemed
to disappear and the countryside took over. The
houses here were no better than the ones in town.
In back of them there were fields of green and yellow
stalks. Jimmy thought they might be corn. He had
seen pictures of corn growing once. The picture had
been bright, cheerful. This wasn't; it was bright,
almost to the point of not having color.

"The white section is built up nice," Crab said.
"They have a Holiday Inn, a lot of new businesses.
It's almost a part of Memphis."

They continued until they reached a row of flat-
roofed buildings that reminded Jimmy of towns he
had seen in westerns. But the people in it didn't
look any different than the people at Mama Jean's
house. Some were standing, some were sitting,
some were leaning against the buildings, but none
of them were going anywhere.

Crab pulled the car over to one of the buildings.
A sign over one window read BLUE LIGHT.

Crab got out quickly, then winced as the pain in
his back got to him. Jimmy got out the other side.

A big man wearing overalls looked at them. He
had one hand in the bib of his overalls. The head-
band of the hat he wore was stained with sweat.

"Morning." Crab nodded.

The man nodded back and quickly looked the
other way down the street as if he shouldn't have
been speaking to a stranger. Crab went to the door
and opened it.

The floor of the Blue Light was wood and uneven.

Jimmy felt his ankles turn slightly, felt how tired his legs were, how tired he was. There was a counter on one side of the room. On the shelves behind it there were bags of meal, rice, and large cans of beans and okra. There was a cash register two-thirds of the way down the counter. On the back wall, beyond the counter, there were bottles of liquor and glasses. Over the bar there was a picture of Martin Luther King next to a picture of Jesus touching a heart that was somehow suspended in front of His chest.

There were four tables on the other side of the large room, and Crab sat down at one of them.

"Not much, huh?" Crab smiled.

Jimmy shrugged.

"When I was a boy," Crab went on, "I used to think the biggest thing to do in the world was to sit in this place or to come to one of the dances they used to have here. Maybe go in the back when nobody was looking and get a drink."

"You used to drink when you were a kid?"

"A little," Crab said. "You don't like that?"

"I just wondered," Jimmy said.

"No, I didn't drink much. Once in a while, if I had a case quarter and there were some girls around or some of the older guys, I'd buy a shot to show how grown I was. Somebody would have it under their coat in the back, and it would be so hot and rough that if you weren't careful it came back up faster than it would go down."

"You were being a man like your father said?" Jimmy said.

Crab didn't answer at first. Jimmy could tell he was thinking about the question, and wondered if he should have asked it.

"Yes," Crab said finally. "Something like that."

A woman came out of the back room, looked over at Crab and Jimmy, then came over.

"Y'all want something to eat?" she asked.

"Give me a couple of scrambled eggs," Crab said. "And you got some slab bacon?"

"No, we got some ham, though."

"Fresh?"

"Yes," she answered. "You from 'round here?"

"I used to live over near The Quarters," Crab said. "I got folks over at Marion."

"Thought I saw you around here," she said. "What you want, baby?"

"Some cereal," Jimmy said.

"We got biscuits," the woman said. "You want some biscuits and some white gravy with a little ham in it?"

Jimmy said okay, that he did, and the woman started walking away.

"You see Rydell much?" Crab called after her.

The woman stopped and turned toward Crab. "He stop by now and then," she said. "You a friend of his?"

"We used to run together," Crab said.

The woman looked at Crab again and then headed toward the back.

Crab went through his pockets until he found a small black address book. He went through it and then showed a name to Jimmy. It read *Rydell Depuis*.

"Give him a call," Crab said. "Tell him I've been looking for the conjure man. Ask him if anybody been around looking for me."

"The *what* man?" Jimmy asked.

Crab pushed the address book toward Jimmy and indicated the phone with a nod.

Jimmy didn't want to make the call. He didn't like to talk to people he didn't know, especially say things to them that he didn't even understand. He wanted to ask Crab what he should say if Rydell asked him who the conjure man was.

He went to the phone, realized he didn't have change for the phone call, and headed back toward Crab. Halfway back he saw Crab go into his pocket and take out the change. Crab put the change on the table.

Jimmy smiled as he took the change. He didn't say anything, and Crab didn't say anything. Crab smiled, though, and that made him feel good.

"Hello?" Jimmy responded to the voice on the other end of the phone. "Is Rydell there?"

"Who's this?"

"Jimmy. Jimmy Little."

Jimmy heard the voice call Rydell. He felt uneasy. He wanted to turn around and see if Crab was looking at him. He didn't. He didn't know why he wanted Crab to think he could do things. Making a telephone call wasn't anything special, but he didn't want to mess it up.

"Hello?" The voice that came through the phone sounded like a hoarse whisper.

"Is this Rydell?"

"Yes, what you want?"

"Crab told me to tell you that he's looking for the conjure man," Jimmy said. "He want to know if anybody looking for him."

"Who?"

"Crab," Jimmy said.

"Crab Little?" The voice rose.

"Yes," Jimmy said, glad that Rydell had recognized Crab's name.

"Where you calling from?"

"A place like . . ." Jimmy looked around. "Like a restaurant. The Blue Light."

"Crab Little is in the Blue Light?"

"Yes."

"Yes, yes." There were moments in which Jimmy could hear the breath of the man on the other end of the line. He listened to it carefully, as if it might tell him something. "Tell him the conjure man is here," the whispery voice answered. "But don't come here starting nothing."

There was a metallic click in the receiver as the phone was hung up on the other end. Jimmy hung up his phone carefully. He turned toward Crab and saw him sitting, head tilted forward, the intense eyes coming from under the high forehead. Crab watched as Jimmy came back to the table.

"He said the conjure man was there," Jimmy said. "He said he was there but that you shouldn't come starting nothing."

Crab nodded.

"Who's the conjure man?" Jimmy asked.

Crab cradled the coffee cup in his fingers and looked down into the dark liquid. "The only place they make worse coffee than here is in Kansas City, Kansas," he said. "I think they have special places they go to learn how to mess up coffee."

Jimmy smiled. "Where we going next?" he asked.

"We got to go see the conjure man," Crab said. "See what he got to say. We don't have a whole lot of time to waste."

"The conjure man might leave?"

"No, he'll be there," Crab said. "But Rydell is going to be checking around. He knows how dirty they did me. Right now he's trying to figure out what I'm doing here. I'll go to the conjure man and get an idea of what kind of time I got to deal with, then I'll know how I got to deal with Rydell."

Crab pushed the plate away from him.

"You ain't hungry?" Jimmy asked.

"I'm *not* hungry," Crab corrected him, smiling. "Say, 'You're *not* hungry.' "

"I guess you're not hungry," Jimmy said.

"You know how long I waited to say something like that?"

"That you ain't hungry?"

"Might have waited too long," Crab said. "Let's go."

"I mean you're *not* hungry," Jimmy said. He looked at Crab and shrugged his shoulders.

"We're getting a few minutes together after all, huh?" Crab said.

He stiffened and grabbed the edge of the table. Then he straightened up.

Jimmy saw the woman who had served them. She was leaning on the counter looking at Crab. She didn't move when she saw his pain. The expression on her face didn't change. Jimmy looked down at the floor for a second, then moved when he noticed Crab starting toward the door.

Crab stopped near the door, took a crumpled five-dollar bill out of his pocket, and put it on the counter near the woman's elbow.

"This cover it?" he asked.

"You didn't like the eggs?" the woman asked,

taking the money. Her hands were fat, her fingers dark swollen stubs that recrumpled the bill into her palm.

"The heat," Crab said. "It takes away your appetite."

"You've been away," the woman said. "You'll get used to it again."

"I hear you," Crab said.

In minutes they were on their way. They hadn't gone more than a mile or so when Jimmy asked when they would get to a service station. "I got to go to the bathroom," he said.

"You need to sit down?"

"No," Jimmy said.

Crab pulled the car over and cut off the motor. Jimmy got out and went behind a tree. As he relieved himself he looked around. It was real country. There were houses that looked like the old houses he had seen in picture books. In the books the houses were supposed to be interesting, or pretty to look at. But these houses had people living in them, men who stood on the front porches with their hands in their pockets. You could never see the hands of the men, Jimmy thought. Sometimes there were women. Sometimes babies crawling in front of the house. There weren't that many cars, and the houses were back from the road.

Jimmy fixed his clothing and got back into the car. Crab started talking as if they had been talking all the while.

"You get sick," he said, "and a conjure man can do you about as much good as a regular doctor. Sometimes more, depending on what you got."

"What you got?" Jimmy asked.

"Just something wrong with my kidneys," Crab said. "It'll pass on by."

"You been to a regular doctor?"

"Sure," Crab said. "I need some rest, some medication. Maybe a good flushing out."

"Rydell sounds funny," Jimmy said.

"Mean voice?"

"Yes."

"He's been working on that mean voice of his since I've known him," Crab said. "Used to play marbles with him when we were kids. You win his marbles and he'd come on with that mean voice trying to get them back. He used to be all right, though. Sometimes I wonder how we would have turned out if things had been different."

"Like what?" Jimmy turned as they passed a mule that was all leather and angles.

"Like if this little thing had happened, or that little thing," Crab said. "I don't know. Maybe if I had the time to think before I got into trouble the same that I had after I got into trouble. Funny thing, they give you all that time in jail to think about your life. When you get out in the street and you can use the time you too busy hustling up a image you can deal with."

"*An* image," Jimmy said. "It's supposed to be *an* image because the next word begins with a vowel."

"We're going to be two English dudes," Crab said, slapping Jimmy on the leg. "Maybe in a little while we'll stop for a spot of tea."

"Maybe," Jimmy said. He felt comfortable, relaxed. He leaned on the headrest as Crab turned on the radio and searched for a station that played the blues.

"You want to stop and get some groceries before we go on to Marion?" Crab asked.

"Sure," Jimmy said. "We going to stay in a hotel in Marion?"

"No," Crab said. "With some people I know."

They drove for almost a half hour, Crab pointing out places he had been when he was a child, Jimmy trying to imagine how Crab looked in the places.

It was almost two when they reached a place called Town and Country Drive-In Service. Crab started to get out of the car, winced, and exhaled sharply as his hands tightened on the steering wheel.

"You want me to go in and get the stuff?" Jimmy asked.

"Yes," Crab answered. "Get some crackers and cheese, stuff like that."

Crab started going through his pockets, and Jimmy pulled up his pants leg and took out the money that Mama Jean had given him. "I got this," he said.

"Where'd you get it?" Crab asked softly.

"Mama Jean."

Crab nodded, went through his pockets, and pulled out some rolled bills. "Hang onto your money in case we need it later," he said.

Jimmy took the money from Crab and went into a store named Quinn's. He thought about Mama Jean while he was in the store. He found a shopping cart, pushed it around the store, and bought cheese, crackers, potato chips, a package of baloney, and a six pack of soda.

He paid for it and saw that he had to put it in the bags himself. The girl working behind the counter was thin; there was a bone that went across the top of her chest that he didn't think he had in his chest. She smiled at him and he smiled back.

He looked out of the window and couldn't see the car. He put the bag down and slipped into the telephone booth. He dialed and waited a long anxious moment before he heard her voice.

"Mama Jean?"

"Jimmy? Is that you, Jimmy?"

"Yes," he said. "We're in Arkansas."

"Arkansas?"

"Uh-huh." Jimmy was glad to hear her voice, glad that she was home. "This is where Crab was when he was little."

"Well, how you doing, baby?"

"I'm doing okay, pretty good," Jimmy said. "I think Crab is sick."

"He don't know you got that money, do he?"

"Yes, he knows," Jimmy said. "He told me to make sure I keep it."

"I was thinking, if you need anything, you can

just call me and I can get it to you by Western
Union," Mama Jean said. "I just think about you all
the time, Jimmy. Do you miss Mama Jean?"

"I can't wait to see you again, Mama Jean," Jimmy
said. "When we get through down here maybe we
can come back to New York and we can all live
together. What you think?"

"We'll see, baby."

"Mama Jean?"

"Jimmy?"

"I got to go now," he said. "I just wanted to call
you to let you know I'm all right and I love you."

"Jimmy . . . baby . . . I love you, too," Mama
Jean said.

" 'Bye now," Jimmy said.

" 'Bye, baby."

There was crying in Mama Jean's voice as she said
good-bye, crying that messed with Jimmy, that
made his chest fill up, and he knew he was close to
crying, too.

He wasn't going to cry. He loved Mama Jean.
God knew he loved Mama Jean, but he was begin-
ning to like Crab, too. Not as much as he liked Mama
Jean, but he was beginning to like him.

When Jimmy got out Crab was standing near the
back of the car.

"I called Mama Jean," Jimmy said.

"What she have to say?" Crab asked.

"Nothing much," Jimmy said. "She wanted to
know how I was doing."

"She say anything about me?"

"I don't think so," Jimmy said. "You know how
she worries sometime."

"I got to get something cool to drink," Crab said. "You got the aspirins?"

"Yes, they in the glove compartment. You got some more pains?"

"No, they still the same old pains," Crab said. "Come on, get the pills and let's go get us a soda."

"We going to lock the stuff I got in the trunk?"

"No, this is Arkansas," Crab said. "You don't have to lock up everything down here. Just leave it in the backseat."

Jimmy put the bag in the backseat and got the aspirins from the glove compartment.

The coolness of the soda shop felt good. There were a group of white kids in one of the booths. One of the boys had a large skull tattooed on his shoulder.

"When I was a kid you couldn't come in here and sit down and have a soda," Crab said as he eased into one of the booths. "You could come in and buy a soda at the counter and take it out, but that was about it."

"They didn't have any seats then?"

Crab looked at Jimmy, then away, then back to him again. "You never heard about segregation?"

"Yes, I heard about it," Jimmy said. He felt slightly hurt by the accusation in Crab's voice.

"What was it?" Crab asked.

"That's when they didn't like Martin Luther King?" Jimmy asked. "Wouldn't let black people vote, stuff like that?"

"It's when they divided the world into white people and niggers," Crab said. "And did little things to make sure you didn't forget which you were.

Things like making you take your soda outside to drink."

Crab's head jerked toward the counter and then quickly away. Jimmy looked over and saw a policeman talking to the man at the cash register. Jimmy tensed.

"You want to leave?" Jimmy asked quietly.

"No," Crab said.

The waitress that took their order for iced tea had pretty eyes and freckles around her nose. The name on her badge read "Spring."

Crab looked at the menu while they waited, and Jimmy wondered if he was nervous about the policeman. When the tea came Jimmy tasted it and found that it wasn't sweetened. He put sugar in it and stirred it with the plastic straw the girl had brought. He saw the policeman go over to the teenagers. The policeman said something that Jimmy didn't hear, and the boy with the tattoo, who had been standing with one foot on the seat of the booth, put his foot down.

The policeman looked around, saw Jimmy looking at him, and came over to them.

"How y'all doing?" He wore a wide leather belt that had two rows of bullets.

"Fine," Jimmy said.

"You from around here?" he asked.

"Forrest," Crab answered. "We've been to New York for the last few years. Visiting relatives in Forrest."

"You must be pretty tough cookies if you can spend a couple of years in New York," the policeman said, looking at Jimmy again.

"I'm not that tough," Jimmy said.

"How about you?" The policeman looked over at Crab. "You must be pretty tough. You come from Forrest and move on up to New York. I been to Forrest and I been to New York. Forrest ain't like no New York."

"Yeah." Crab looked down at his tea.

"Don't y'all New York boys get in no trouble over in Forrest, now," the policeman said. He turned, nodded toward the clerk at the register, and left.

They finished the iced teas and Jimmy paid for them. Crab went to the rest room, and Jimmy stood at the door waiting for him. He seemed to take a long time, and the man at the register kept looking at Jimmy. Jimmy smiled and the man looked away.

Crab came out of the rest room and they went to the car. Jimmy looked in the backseat and saw that the bag was still there.

"I need to get some more exercise," Crab said.

They pulled out of the shopping center past a sign that read *THIS IS AMERICA — I love it — if you don't — get the hell out!*

"There aren't many people here — "

Crab held up his hand to silence Jimmy. He looked in the rearview mirror.

"He's following us," Crab said.

"Who?"

"That policeman back in the soda shop," Crab said.

"He after you?"

"No," Crab said. "I don't think so. If you're from out of town down here they're suspicious. He'll follow me awhile, make sure I'm going where I said I was going, then turn off."

"Where'd you say we were going?"

"Forrest," Crab said, glancing into the rearview mirror again. "Just wanted to let him know I knew the area. Down here they'd rather see a snake than a stranger."

Crab slowed the car down to the speed limit and showed Jimmy the sights. He told him which homes were new, which were old but looked new, and which were old when they were first built.

"People get some old wood and build any kind of place they can. If they find a foundation already built, I mean a good foundation, which is cement sunk into the ground, or even pilings that's really sunk and haven't had too much water damage, then they got something.

"You either build something or listen to the cities calling you."

"What you mean?" Jimmy was turned halfway around in the seat. He could look back and see the gray-blue car that Crab had said was following them. It stayed in the same lane they were in.

"You get yourself a piece of money and you want to go out and put up a house somewhere around here," Crab said. "But you keep hearing the call of the city."

"What it say?"

"What it say?" Crab looked over at Jimmy. "It says 'Come on over here and get this big money job and sit in the bright lights and dream you a white folks' dream.'

"And for all your knowing that it's not true it just sounds too sweet to pass on."

"Is that what happened to you?" Jimmy asked. "That's how you got to the city?"

"No, I didn't have any money," Crab said. "I went

into the army, found out other people didn't live like black people here live and just couldn't satisfy myself to staying here."

"He's still following us," Jimmy said.

"Yes, well, if he knowed anything he'd be pulling up on us," Crab said.

"Then what happened?"

"Then he'd pull us over and tell us to get out of the car," Crab said.

"No." Jimmy shook his head. "I mean, after you left here. What happened then?"

"Found all the excuses I needed," Crab said. "And got satisfied with them."

"Here he comes," Jimmy said, turning back toward the front of the car.

"Just smile nice at him," Crab said. "He probably wants to take one more look before he turns off."

The unmarked police car pulled alongside, and Crab waved and smiled so that the policeman could see his teeth. The policeman nodded, waved, and pulled ahead. He turned off the next exit, and Crab went on until he found a U-turn.

"You knew just what he was going to do," Jimmy said.

"All I did was to know how to deal with the police," Crab said. "What are you smiling about?"

Jimmy shrugged. Crab seemed suddenly angry. It was as if he had said something that had made Crab mad. But he didn't know what it could have been.

For a while Jimmy had thought that he was beginning to know Crab. He had liked sitting with him in the car, just the two of them, talking about things that Crab had done years before. He had liked it when Crab was right about what the policeman was going to do, too. In a funny way he had even liked it because Crab was hurting. Now, as the miles droned by, they were right where they had been before. Crab was a stranger, and here, far away from Mama Jean and home, so was he.

"We're coming up on Marion now," Crab announced after what had seemed forever. "Over there you can see a good farm. See how black the soil is. There's no dust on it. When you get dust on the soil it means it's no good. All you grow — look over there — look how the wind blows the dust up."

Jimmy looked and saw a small swirl of dust lift up from the ground and settle quickly down again. On the other place, where the dirt was black, the house and small buildings were white, with dark red trim. On the place where the dust swirled, the buildings were gray on top and the same as the dust on the bottom. It was as if the dust were pulling the buildings down.

There was a cluster of buildings, some wooden and some brick, and they slowed down as they passed them. A few black people waved to them. The white people looked at the Illinois license plate and watched without recognition as the car passed.

"I know some of these people," Crab said. "I can't call their names off the top of my head but I know them."

He pulled the car over to the curb, stopped it quickly, and threw it into reverse. He started backing down the street until he came to the corner. Jimmy looked down the street and saw the policeman that had been following them. He was standing near his car, his back toward them, drinking a soda.

"He doubled back on us," Crab said as he eased the car backward around the corner.

He turned the car around and moved the car down the street and parked behind a stand of cypress trees.

Crab said that they were still in Marion, but the place they went to was not a place the way that Jimmy knew places. It was just a few buildings here and there; Jimmy didn't even want to call them houses.

"Suppose he comes out here?" Jimmy asked.

"He's not coming out here," Crab said.

A moment later they saw the policeman's car pull away, and Crab started up again. There were angry rain clouds above and the sky darkened. Crab switched on the lights. They drove for nearly ten minutes, going from one cluster of houses to another, before stopping at one of them.

"This is called 'The Quarters,'" Crab said.

Jimmy could see people sitting on the porch of the house they had stopped near. Jimmy got out of the car when he saw Crab getting out.

"Who that, Taylor?" A low woman's voice came through the darkness.

"No, it's me, Crab."

"Crab? Crab Little?" the voice responded. "Jesse, bring out the lamp." A door opened and a thin girl came out holding a floor lamp. She put it down and turned it on.

Crab stepped up on the porch. He was holding his head to one side and smiling. "Now don't tell me you ain't got no mustard greens in the pot," he said.

"Yes, we got some. . . . Jesse, go fix up some plates. Who's this?"

"This is my boy," Crab said. "Mine and Dolly's."

"Well, do tell!" The woman wore a wig that came down over one side of her forehead. "Jesse, fix two plates. I'm out here trying to catch a little breeze."

"Looks like rain," Crab said.

"It ain't gonna rain," the woman said. "It ain't rained enough to give a ladybug a decent shower since last winter. What's your boy's name?"

"Lord, I'm sorry. Miss Mackenzie, this is Jimmy. Jimmy, this is Miss Mackenzie."

"Hello, ma'am."

"Well, hello to you," Miss Mackenzie said.

"We been traveling near all day," Crab said.

"You must have wanted to get here bad to travel all day in this heat," she answered. "You heard Reverend Brown died?"

"O. C. Brown?"

"No, he *been* gone. I mean Reverend Louis Brown, used to be at Bethel up in Marianna. Man, I forgot how long you been away from here."

"Yes, been a while," Crab said.

"I'm glad you ain't forgot us," Miss Mackenzie said. "Seems like most of the world don't know we even down here. My sister said she saw a map and they left Basset completely off. Now ain't that something?"

"Sure is."

"Why don't you get a load off your feet?"

"We got to make a quick run tonight," Crab said, pulling some money out of his pocket. "Then we looking for a room for maybe a couple of days."

"You know you can always stay here," the woman said. "Where you going to run to?"

"We got to go see the conjure man," Crab said. "Got to check out a few things with him."

"Well, you know where he stays," Miss Mackenzie said.

Jesse fixed two plates of greens, sliced pork, and potato salad. Crab and Jimmy ate in the kitchen. They had an old stove with "Black Diamond" printed on the front. The tablecloth had snowmen and Christmas trees on it.

Jesse looked about Jimmy's age. A beautiful girl with clear black skin and eyes that looked almost Oriental, she hadn't spoken since they had arrived. Jimmy saw her looking at him, though. There was a square space between the kitchen and the living room. There were curtains on the living room side, and Jimmy could see the girl, her image softened by the flickering light from candles that stood on either side of a book Jimmy figured was probably a Bible. In the soft light Jimmy thought that the girl looked like a black angel. He thought of his mother.

"What's the conjure man like?" Jimmy asked.

"He's a kind of doctor," Crab said. "I told you that before."

"Oh, that's right," Jimmy said.

Crab ate slowly, and Jimmy did, too. Jimmy didn't realize how hungry he had been. When he finished eating the greens and pork he was still hungry, but he didn't say anything.

The girl was still looking at him. Even when they were finished and were leaving to go to the conjure man he felt her looking at him, even though he didn't see her.

The conjure man's house was set off from the others. There were boards placed over the steps to make a kind of ramp. Jimmy couldn't see much of the house in the darkness. A brilliant white half-moon hung sullenly in the night sky above the point of the tin roof. His feet slid in the sandy soil around the bottom of the darkened porch.

Crab stopped. Jimmy expected him to call out, but he didn't. He just waited in the darkness. Jimmy looked up at Crab and saw the whites of his eyes wider than he had ever seen them before. Jimmy stepped closer to him.

"Who's there?" The voice was flat, dry as the dirt they stood on.

"It's me, Crab!"

"Who you want to see?"

"High John!"

"Come on."

Crab moved forward and Jimmy went with him, staying as close as he could without touching. They moved to the steps and up them. A sliver of light to their right widened into a door, and Jimmy let Crab go in before him.

"Been a while, Crab," High John said.

"Yeah."

"I know you sick," High John said. "Sit down. You want some tea?"

"Don't mind if I do," Crab said. "I don't have too much to give you."

"When did that matter to me?" High John spoke the words in a low voice as he turned away toward the stove. "People forget High John. They take their dollars down to the city clinic to people who don't care if they live or die. You think those people know that people got souls?"

"Sometimes I wonder," Crab said.

High John took the water off the stove and poured it into a blue enamel cup. He took another cup from behind the stove and put that one next to the first.

"The boy drink tea?"

"No," Jimmy said.

High John poured the water into the second cup. The room was filled with the strange, sweet smell of it. He was a small man, and old. His face was as dark as black walnuts, and deeply lined. But however old the face was, however lined and worn with age, the eyes were older.

The light from the small lamp on the edge of the table flickered in his dark pupils as he sat. He lifted the cup to his lips and closed his eyes as he drank.

"Put the money on the bed," he said when he had finished drinking.

Crab got up and walked across the room. There was a quilt on the bed and Crab put the money on it. Then he came back to the table and began to drink the tea that High John had set out for him.

"You come home to get the boy?" High John asked.

"I brought him with me from New York," Crab said.

"Glad you brought the boy here," High John said. "A man finds peace in his sons, and a woman finds life in her daughters. It's a right thing to do, isn't it?"

Crab looked over at Jimmy. "You saying it, High John."

"It's a right thing to do," High John said. He had sat at the end of the table away from Crab. He cupped the tea in his hands and held it close to him. The steam from the tea shimmered in front of his face. "You come home to see where you come from, and to see what has come from you."

"I got questions to ask you, High John," Crab said.

"You don't have to ask me nothing," High John said. "When you come from as far away as you done come from you already got the answers. There's a veil and a cloud. Sometimes a child is born with a veil over its eyes and it can see the other side. Sometimes a man grows a cloud over his eyes and can't see the work of his own hand, or the truth in his own heart."

Silence. For a long time, silence. For a time that grew weight and lay before them on the wooden table, silence. Then Jimmy heard the humming sound of a lazy fan in the next room, and beyond that the softer buzz of life beyond the window.

A grasshopper landed on the table, its body as

fragile as the moment, its form as still as the silence that lay between the three of them.

The humming of the fan faded gradually from his attention, which was taken over by the grasshopper. It changed position, the thin lines moving improbably along the table toward a shallow copper dish. It stopped, almost invisible in the dim light.

Crab spoke.

"I was away, High John. I was in prison. And I left everything I had there. I just came to Marion to clear things up."

Crab stopped, his head down, his chest heaving.

"Go on, son," High John said.

"I've been sick for more than a while . . ."

Crab stopped again, his words weighed down by the silence that followed. His hand shook as he drank from the cup.

High John got up and went around the table to the bed. He spread the quilt out.

"That quilt was made way back in the hard times before the Civil War. Can't think of what could have made them make something so pretty. Can't think of where they could get the prettiness from. Maybe that's the only things old High John is waiting around this earth to find out. I don't know. Sometimes I think it is, sometimes I think it's not.

"Come here and rest yourself," High John said, patting the quilt.

Crab stood up and went to the bed. He lay down on it and crossed his hands over his stomach.

"Where your pain?" High John asked.

"Here," Crab said, touching the small of his back on the side.

Jimmy watched, seeing for the first time how small High John was, how he was mostly body with small legs and arms.

High John touched Crab's back, and Jimmy heard a gasp.

"Boy, bring that lamp over here." High John pointed behind him.

Jimmy didn't realize at first that he was talking to him, then realized it and jumped. He got the lamp and brought it to High John.

"Close your eyes." High John whispered the words to Crab.

Crab closed his eyes and High John pulled back the lids. Jimmy, standing at the end of the bed, lifted his head to see over High John's arm. He saw Crab's eyes; they were mostly yellow. Jimmy thought it must have been from the reflection of the lamp.

"Can you breathe deep?"

Crab breathed in as deeply as he could. Jimmy breathed in, too. He wanted to breathe for Crab, to suck in the warm night air, to suck in half of Arkansas if need be.

"This is going to hurt a bit," the old man said.

He traced a finger along Crab's arms and into the armpit. He pushed and Crab's whole body quivered. Crab reached for High John's arms, then stopped himself. High John nodded and wet his lips.

"Come finish your tea," he said.

He turned and went back to the table and sat where he had sat before. Crab got up slowly. He looked at Jimmy and patted him on his arm.

"You ain't never seen a conjure man before, have you?"

"No," Jimmy said, relieved at Crab's smile.

"Where you staying?" High John asked Crab.

"Over at Miss Mackenzie's," Crab said.

"I ever tell you I almost married that woman?" High John said.

"Get out of here!"

"Yeah, 'bout fifty years ago. When was the War in Europe? 'Round that time. She was married to a man named Harrison Redwood. Half the black people around here was named Redwood in those days. Anyway, he was in the navy and went out to Puget Sound, Washington. So they tell me they had to take a ferry from the navy base to town. He got drunk one night and fell off the ferry and drowned. She was all upset and big-legged and I almost married her."

"Why didn't you?"

"I asked myself why I needed to marry a woman bigger than me, stronger than me, and who kept saying no when I asked her to marry me. Couldn't find no reason, so I gave her up!"

High John chuckled, and Jimmy saw that he didn't have many teeth. He glanced over at Crab, and Crab was smiling. Jimmy smiled, too.

Crab sat back down at the table and finished his tea. Jimmy looked for the grasshopper. It was gone.

"You drink you as much sassafras tea as you can stand," High John said. "That'll give you some relief. Don't make it with no fresh-grown bark, though. That'll mess you up good."

"I appreciate it," Crab said.

Jimmy saw the grasshopper. It was on the windowsill. Then it was gone into the night.

High John opened his refrigerator and took out a

small red can of snuff. He opened it and put some in his mouth, sticking his tongue out to receive it and then rolling it into the side of his mouth.

Crab was standing.

"I think I should get some rest," he said.

They walked to the front door and outside. The night air was cooler than Jimmy remembered it. There was a little breeze. High John walked them to the edge of the porch.

"So what you think?" Crab asked, softly.

"You walking in strength, Crab," High John said. "But only you and the Good Lord know where you getting it from."

They said good-bye to High John and walked slowly back toward Miss Mackenzie's. Jimmy turned back toward High John's cabin and saw the tree, its leafy branches eerie against the moon that was lower than it had been.

Crab didn't speak all the way over. Jimmy tried to think about what had happened at High John's and whether it was good or bad. He sensed that it was not good.

They got to Miss Mackenzie's and she was asleep on the porch with the radio on. A guitar strained a tinny blues through the cheap radio speaker so that it sounded vaguely foreign. Crab reached over and turned it off. Miss Mackenzie woke up.

"Oh, I wasn't sleeping," she said. "Just resting my eyes from the ragweed. You know it's a shame the way I suffer from the ragweed."

"Yeah, it's bad this time of year," Crab said.

"They got it growing wild down near the railroad tracks," Miss Mackenzie said. "Somebody should go

down there and just burn it down. It's higher than
a full-grown man!"

"I hear that," Crab said.

"Y'all go on in the back room past the stairs," she
said. "Jesse got it fixed up nice for you. You want
me to get you up in the morning?"

"Tired as we are you might have to fight us to get
us up," Crab said.

"And, child, you know I'm too old to be fighting,"
Miss Mackenzie said, laughing.

Jimmy had to go to the bathroom and Crab told
him where it was.

Jimmy had heard of outdoor bathrooms and the
flashlight that Miss Mackenzie gave him made it
easy for him to find it. It smelled terrible. He used
it quickly, then looked for a way to flush it. There
wasn't any. He didn't want to look down into the
hole, but did anyway. It was further down than he
thought, and the smell made him leave before he
got a really good look.

When he got to the room Crab was already in
bed. The room smelled of cocoa butter, and Jimmy
thought it was probably the room Miss Mackenzie
usually slept in.

"Night," Jimmy said.

"Night," Crab answered.

"How did that guy get to be a conjure man?"
Jimmy asked.

"Some people just got it in them, I guess," Crab
said. "I don't really know. Some people have the
gift handed down to them from the olden times.
They know things."

"What kind of things?"

"Things that other people don't know," Crab said.
"Like what?"

"I don't know," Crab said, a trace of annoyance
in his voice.

Jimmy pulled the sheet up to his chin. The light
flickered, and he turned to see Crab trying to reach
the switch. Crab put two thin fingers on the body
of the lamp and grasped the chain with the others.

In the darkness Jimmy pulled the sheet up to his
nose.

High John was strange when you thought about
him, calling him a conjure man and such, but he
didn't look particularly strange, Jimmy thought, just
old. He thought about High John as a baby, being
born with a veil over his eyes. He wondered what
his mother must have thought.

Jimmy thought he was going to be scared, but he
wasn't. He was tired, though. His legs were aching.
Before he fell asleep he thought of Mama Jean, then
he thought of some of the kids in his class. He wondered what they had said when he had stopped
coming to school. Probably just thought he was a
dropout or something.

He didn't remember falling asleep. The noise he
heard that woke him up was, in the middle of his
dream, a wild terrifying sound that made his heart
race. For a moment he couldn't remember where
he was. Then he did and, not knowing what the
noise was, he was afraid. He listened carefully. It
was somebody crying.

He pulled the sheet down from his face and saw
that it was just begining to grow light outside. The
crying sounded as if it were in the room with him,
as if it were coming from Crab's bed.

Jimmy sat up slowly and turned toward where he could see Crab curled in a tight knot. He didn't know what to do. He thought maybe Crab was sick and needed help. He got up and stepped onto the cold floor.

"Crab?" he said softly.

The sobs, too, came softly.

He went to the bed and looked at Crab. His eyes were closed. He wasn't crying at the moment, but his face was wet. Jimmy looked at him breathing, saw how deep the breaths were, and knew that he was still asleep. He had been crying in his sleep.

He went back to his own bed and covered himself with the sheet.

What could Crab have been dreaming about, he thought, that was so sad? For some reason, he didn't know why, he thought of him being in prison. He wondered if, locked in a cell, in the darkness, he had cried there, too.

He told himself to go back to sleep, but he couldn't. He hoped that Crab wouldn't cry again. He was sorry that he had heard him.

He hadn't ever thought of a man crying before. If anybody had asked him he would have said a man could cry if he was hurt, or maybe if he was sad. But it was nothing that he had ever thought about before.

He hadn't thought, either, in the times that he had thought about having his father around, that his father would ever cry. He had thought about a man being strong, and knowing things and telling him things. He had never dreamed of a man lying in a strange bed and tearing the gray hollow of a new day with his tears. He knew, back in Chicago, that

Crab had never thought of his son not being tough, not being able to handle some kid like Frank. But Frank had been tougher than Jimmy was, tougher inside and bigger outside. Jimmy knew he couldn't have handled Frank. And now, down in Arkansas, back home like High John had said, Crab had found something tougher than he was and he couldn't handle it.

Crab turned in his bed and made another sound. It wasn't crying, but it was close. Jimmy thought that when he woke up he would ask him what High John had meant.

Morning came with a scorch of white heat that
pushed the people of Marion out of their houses and
onto their porches. In the house down from Miss
Mackenzie's, two boys pulled an overstuffed chair
onto the porch and a frail woman came to sit on it.
The distant sky was white, and the birds that circled
and swooped against it were black. In one corner of
the porch there was a picture of Martin Luther King,
cut out from a magazine and framed.

On the side of the house flies buzzed in erratic
patterns over the full garbage can. Miss Mackenzie
came out onto the stoop and put her arm around
Jimmy's shoulders.

"Going to be a long, hot day," she said.

"Looks like it," Jimmy said. The words came out
naturally, as if he had said them before.

A small girl came from somewhere. Jimmy
thought her to be about four or five. Her skin was
dark, black almost, but her hair was black in spots
and orange in other spots. She was skinny, too,
except for her stomach, which pushed the green

dress out in front till her underwear could be seen under the buttons. The dress fit poorly at the shoulders and went down too far on the thin legs. She carried a white doll with blonde hair. She saw Jimmy and held the doll up to him, then laughed and brought it to her chest and hugged it.

"She love that doll," Miss Mackenzie said. "Love it like it was a real baby."

The girl held the baby toward Jimmy again, taunting him with it. Jimmy looked at her for a moment more, then let his mind drift to Crab.

He hadn't realized before that he had been a little afraid of Crab. But after seeing him at High John's house, after hearing the sobs come from the tightly curled body, he wasn't afraid of him anymore.

The girl, sensing that Jimmy wasn't paying her attention, ran away.

The screen door closed behind him, and he could feel the porch boards move under him. Jimmy turned and saw Crab move across the porch and lean on the railing. That was Crab's style. To show up and let you look at him, make what you want of how he looked or who he was.

"How you doing?" Jimmy asked.

"You want some eggs?" Miss Mackenzie asked before Crab had answered Jimmy.

"Could use some coffee," Crab said.

Miss Mackenzie went by Crab, stopping to touch him on the chest.

"I'm calling on Rydell today," Crab said when the last of Miss Mackenzie's dress had disappeared into the house. "I want you to come with me."

"Okay," Jimmy said.

He followed Crab's gaze out over the flat barren land. In the distance shimmering heat waves danced through dust swirls along the edge of the road.

"We too far from the water," Crab said. "Ain't nothing around here got a life of its own. You go down toward the river and you'll find a little creek with a bridge over it. Sometimes you can catch some fish over there, catfish mostly, and you can see water bugs along the shore. Sometimes I used to go over there just to see something living besides the folks. That's a nice little creek; it ain't big enough to make a difference for growing things, but it's a nice little creek."

"You know about growing things?" Jimmy asked.

"Not enough," Crab said.

Miss Mackenzie came out with a small tray. There was a cup of coffee on it for Crab and some lemonade for Jimmy.

"I'm going over to Marianna today," Miss Mackenzie said. "Mr. Logan is going to pick me up. Probably stop at Will May's and pick up some things."

"They still keep the lights out there when it gets hot?" Crab asked, wrapping his fingers around the cup until the tips touched on the other side.

"No, those tube lights don't get hot like the old ones did." Miss Mackenzie wiped her hands on her apron. "They use tube lights now."

The lemonade was warm and thin.

"Here comes Rydell!" Jesse called down from the second-floor window.

Jimmy glanced up toward Jesse and then turned and looked for Rydell. He didn't see anything.

"Where is he, Jesse?" Miss Mackenzie called out.

"Passing over near Mr. Horn's well. I think he coming from Cypress Lane."

Miss Mackenzie looked and then pointed. Jimmy saw a car coming in the distance.

"How do you know it's Rydell?" Crab called up to her.

"He the only one got a blue car like that and come from that direction," Jesse said.

They watched as the car came closer.

"Why don't you go in with Jesse, Miss Mackenzie?" Crab handed Miss Mackenzie the cup.

"There going to be trouble?" Miss Mackenzie asked.

"He ain't looking for trouble from me," Crab said. "He just knows I'm looking to talk to him."

Jimmy watched Crab pull up a wooden crate from the side of the porch and put his foot on it.

Rydell's Cadillac seemed to sag as it moved along the road. He turned it toward the house, then back toward the road, stopping when the driver's side was near the porch. The back window was cracked and the chrome grill rusted on one side.

Rydell didn't look at them as he took a cigar from the dashboard and slowly lit it. Jimmy looked at Crab and saw him smiling.

The cigar lit, Rydell opened the door of the big car and got out slowly. His long hair was thick and slicked down against his head, ending in tight curls on the back of his neck. The hair in the small goatee he wore was just as thick but flecked with gray. From where he stood Jimmy could see the lacquered nails as Rydell flicked ashes on the ground.

Rydell Depuis's broad shoulders sloped against the rounded top of the Cadillac as he leaned against it and crossed his legs at the ankle.

They looked like dangerous men, Jimmy thought, Crab with his weight on one knee, Rydell in his collarless shirt, a gold medallion hanging low on his chest.

"So, old Big City Crab is home again?" Rydell said, quietly. "You here for a while, or you just passing through?"

"Ain't made my mind up yet," Crab said, scratching under his chin. "Thought maybe I'd check out some things, do a little talking with some old friends, and see how things are laying."

"What kind of things you want to talk about?" Rydell asked.

"You take a long fall like I took — a long fall for nothing — you got a lot of things to talk about," Crab said. "Thought maybe somebody owe me something on that account."

"You talking mysteries, my man." Rydell lifted his shoulders as he spoke. "Maybe I don't understand that big city talk."

"Thought homeboys always understood each other," Crab said. "Least we used to understand each other more than we understood what the Man had to say."

"You been talking to the Man?" Rydell asked.

"Ain't got around to it yet."

Rydell looked at his cigar, tried to puff on it, and then reached into his pocket for his matches. He found them, lit one, and stuck the end of his cigar in the small flame and sucked on it until the tip glowed a dull orange.

"I heard you were here looking for the conjure man," Rydell said. "I didn't think you were here looking to start no mess."

"Ain't looking to start nothing," Crab said. "Just thought I could sit down with a homeboy over a jug of something sweet and deal with some truth about what happened."

"Big city boy like you come all the way out here to talk some truth?" Rydell asked. "Must be a powerful truth you talking these days."

"It is," Crab said.

Jimmy watched Crab stand and move to the rail. His neck looked puffed up, and Jimmy wondered if he was hurting.

An open-bed truck passed on the road. The white man in the front seat next to the driver was shirtless, with dark arms and a white chest that looked even whiter in the dingy cab.

"So what you want from me?" Rydell held the cigar loosely in his hand.

"You know I wasn't in on that armored car," Crab said, his voice getting stronger.

"How I know that?" Rydell looked at the cigar. "I wasn't there."

"Then why you split in such a hurry?"

"They put you in jail for killing the guard." Rydell looked up at the window where Jesse had been. "You say you didn't do it, but they still put you in jail. If you didn't do anything and they put you in jail they were liable to put me in jail, too, because I didn't do nothing."

"I guess we got to deal with each other," Crab said. "I guess that's what it gets down to."

"I ain't looking for trouble, Crab." Rydell shifted

his weight from one foot to the other and back. "I don't even know why you come back here. I ain't got nothing for you to come back here for."

"I brought my boy here so he could hear the truth," Crab said. "And I mean for him to hear it."

"That you didn't do nothing?"

"That I didn't kill nobody," Crab said.

Rydell shifted uneasily and looked over at Jimmy. "You got a clear walk, or you on parole?" he asked.

"I'm on parole," Crab said. "Told the Man I could get work in West Memphis."

"Don't sound right to me, man." Rydell shook his head. "Don't sound right."

"I'm here, ain't I?"

"How I know you're not here looking for me to say something you can carry back to the Man?"

"Why would I come back here to do something like that?" Crab said.

"Yeah, why?" Rydell's eyes narrowed until they closed. He lifted his chin and traced one finger from his goatee down the front of his throat until he reached the chain he wore. He nodded slowly, as if he had come to some decision. Then he opened his eyes and looked at Crab.

"You begging, man," he said. "I don't know what you begging for, but you begging. A man travel all the way across the country to get nowhere and don't have nothing to say is begging. What you begging for?"

"I'm not begging," Crab said. "I'm looking for the truth."

"No. No." Rydell shook his head as he opened the door of the Cadillac. "You begging and I got to figure out what you begging for."

"I'll deal with you, Rydell." Crab's voice raised in anger. "I'll deal with you!"

"Yeah, maybe." Rydell started the car. "And I'll give your search for 'truth' some real hard thought."

Rydell put the cigar in his mouth, took it out, and turned the Cadillac away from the house.

The car crunched the dry earth beneath its tires, earth that hadn't given anything of itself for a hundred hard summers, and rolled eastward toward West Memphis.

Crab had gone down the porch steps and now took a hesitant step in the direction of the car, and another, lifting one arm as if to pull it back, then dropping it to his side.

Jimmy had to wet his lips before speaking. "Crab?"

"Yeah?"

"I don't think you . . . you know . . . did it," Jimmy said.

"You sure I didn't?" Crab asked.

Jimmy started thinking about it, trying to figure out what to say to Crab. He searched for words, looked into Crab's eyes for them, opening his mouth hoping they would be there, standing soundlessly as Crab finally turned away.

"Crab, I'm sorry," he said.

"I'll have to deal with Rydell," Crab said. "Some people need the truth pried out of them."

"What are you going to do?" Jimmy asked.

Crab looked up to the sky. The sun was high, but the heat seemed to come from the ground. Miss Mackenzie came out onto the porch with a small basket of snap beans.

"Everything all right, Crab?" she asked.

"Yeah, everything's all right," Crab said.

Miss Mackenzie put the basket of snap beans next to the chair leg. Then she went back into the house for a moment before reappearing with a brown sack, which she put on the other side of the chair. She sat, spread her legs, and made a well by pushing her dress down between heavy thighs. She took a handful of beans and began to snap them with her fingers into the right size for cooking. The ends she dropped into the sack. The fingers worked quickly, expertly, as they had a thousand times before.

"That creek still clean?" Crab half turned toward Miss Mackenzie.

"I guess it's clean," Miss Mackenzie said. "You think Rydell means you some trouble?"

"No, he don't mean nothing to me," Crab said, turning to Jimmy. "I'm going to take Jimmy down the creek a while and just forget Rydell. You want to go on down there a while?"

"Okay."

"You know that Rydell can be a snake when he want to be," Miss Mackenzie said as they started off.

"Yeah, I know," Crab said. He sounded tired. "C'mon, Jimmy."

He walked slowly, like an old man, Jimmy thought. Jimmy walked next to him, picked up the awkward rhythm, tried to see if there was pain in Crab's face without seeming to look.

"You used to come down to the creek when you were a kid?"

"Used to live at the creek," Crab said. "Sometimes, when it was too hot to sleep in the house,

I'd come on down to the creek with my pillow. I used to think it was a big thing, to have a pillow. Around here you had to be grown to get a pillow. Ain't that something? Those were some times."

"What he says . . ." Jimmy said. "What Rydell says doesn't mean anything."

"Yes, it does," Crab said softly.

The creek was a half mile away from the house. The meadow that had been there years before had given way to barrenness. The trees along the way were less grand, less green. A discarded sink, stained brown from years of rusty water, touched the edge of the creek. They walked along the creek as it widened somewhat, the clear water making Vs over the rocks and old bottles alike.

Jimmy picked up a stick and dragged it along the edge of the creek.

"The creek was knee deep here once," Crab said. "It really was a creek then."

"What was your mother like?" Jimmy asked. "She was my grandmother."

"A good black woman," Crab said. "You would have liked each other. You want to rest a while?"

"No, I'm not . . . yeah, sure," Jimmy said, remembering that Crab might not be feeling well. "You want me to go get those aspirins?"

"No," Crab answered. Jimmy watched Crab go over to a low tree, put his back against it, and slide slowly to the ground. The tree leaned away from Crab, and he closed his eyes as he rested his head against it.

"I could go get you a hat from Miss Mackenzie," Jimmy said.

"I'm okay," Crab said. "Just need to rest a while."

He closed his eyes again, and Jimmy saw that his face looked swollen.

"You walking in strength, Crab," High John had said. *"But only you and the Good Lord know where you getting it from."*

"Suppose." Jimmy pushed one end of the stick he had been dragging in the creek and pushed it into the dirt. "Suppose Rydell had said that you didn't do nothing. What would happen then?"

"Then maybe my prison dreams would come true," Crab said. "That's all I got. Prison dreams of starting over, and getting land. In prison all your dreams start with 'If.' If this could happen, if you could start all over again. Rydell was supposed to say that I didn't kill the guard, and you would hear it and feel great or something. Then we'd walk off together into the sunset."

"Like cowboys?"

"Yeah, like cowboys," Crab said. "When I was a kid we used to go to the movies when we had the money — we'd walk all the way to make the whole thing last longer — and sit up in the balcony with the black people. They used to call it the 'Colored' section back in them days. Anyway, they would have a cowboy movie, and all the black kids up in the balcony would be imagining they were the hero and all the white kids downstairs would imagine the same thing. The dreaming got so good you couldn't tell it from real. I guess I had prison dreams even before I got to prison."

"He could have just said it," Jimmy said.

"Yeah," Crab said. "He could have. But one thing a gutter rat hates is to see another gutter rat sitting in the sun."

"That's a funny thing to say." Jimmy pushed his stick under a small rock, tipping it over, then jumped back as he saw a nest of slugs under the rock. He looked to see if Crab had seen him jump and saw that he had.

They smiled and Jimmy shrugged.

The slugs moved slowly, crawling over and around each other, then disappeared into the soft mud.

"So now what?" Jimmy asked.

"I don't know." The words came out softly, almost in a whisper. "Maybe stay here a while and see how Rydell acts. If he tells the truth — like he's supposed to — maybe everything will be all right. If he don't then we'll just have to see. I was thinking about going to California. You ever see California?"

If I already believe it, why does Rydell have to say it, too? Jimmy formed the words carefully in his mind. "Why Rydell got to say it?" was the way it came out.

" 'Cause I want things to be right with us," Crab said. "Take an easy drive out to California and start fresh. They say the sea air is good for you. Little sea, little sun. Who knows? Might start feeling like a kid again."

"How you feeling now?"

"Tired," Crab said. He pushed to his feet slowly, steadied himself, waiting until his breath returned to normal from the effort, then started walking along the edge of the creek. Jimmy followed at a distance.

California wasn't what Jimmy had wanted Crab to say. He didn't know what it was that he did want him to say but it wasn't California, and it wasn't renting another car. He thought about being in the hotel lobby back in Chicago, seeing Crab give the girl a credit card with somebody else's name on it. He remembered having breakfast and the policeman asking about the first car that Crab had brought to Mama Jean's house. California wasn't what he wanted to hear.

Maybe, he thought, what he had been thinking was like what Crab had been dreaming, just prison dreams. He had been thinking, since that moment in the hall when he had first seen him, his mind racing wildly through scenes of family and wholeness, that maybe something magical would happen. It wouldn't have been walking off into the sunset. It would have been about him and Crab together and knowing something special that could never be forgotten.

Crab stopped ahead of him and knelt down. He was looking at something in the mud. Jimmy walked up and stood over him to see what he was doing. It was just a worm, long and red. Crab stuck a finger under it and pushed it up and watched it try to hide itself again. Jimmy thought Crab would leave the worm alone but he pushed a finger into the mud and pulled it up again. Jimmy watched him, looked at him kneeling in the mud. He looked away, holding Crab in his mind closer than he had ever been to him, thought about the dark hands, fingers wider at the ends than in the middle, nails yellowed and bent, pushing into the mud.

"When we were kids we used to come out here after a good rain and get a can full of these suckers," Crab said. "Then we'd fish with them."

"Catch many fish?" Jimmy asked.

"Not around here," Crab said. "You had to go to

the river to really catch anything. We'd fish here because we were here, not because we'd catch anything."

"You want to go back to New York?" Jimmy asked. "We could stay with Mama Jean."

"How long you think it would take them to come looking for me there?" Crab asked, his voice hard-edged.

"So what are we going to do?" Jimmy asked, trying to keep his voice from cracking. "We can't just keep going around, you know, getting cars and things."

"Give me a break," Crab said. "I'm trying to think of something."

No. The tears stung Jimmy's eyes and broke the harshness of the day into a thousand soft lights that danced and shimmered in front of him. He heard Crab saying something about being tough, about keeping himself together. Jimmy started to say that he would, but the words stuck in his throat and came out a weak gurgle. The moment of holding Crab in his mind was going, he could feel it slip away. He looked at Crab, searching the unreal silhouette of him, dark against the parched yellow reeds and the white distant sky, and looked for someone he loved, and all he saw was the darkness of the man, the outstretched hand, the stark face and the starker gash that was the open silent mouth. He started to walk away. He felt Crab's hand on his shoulder and he lifted his arm and jerked his shoulder away. He walked away quickly, into the tall grass that made swishing noises against his legs.

"Jimmy! Jimmy!" Crab called to him. "Man, don't be that way!"

Jimmy turned to see Crab hurrying after him, his

hand outstretched, fingers wide. "Jimmy!"

"It don't make a difference if you didn't kill anybody," Jimmy said. "Not if you're going to steal some money or credit cards or something. That's wrong, too. It don't make you good just because you didn't kill nobody!"

"Sure it does. Sure it does." Crab took Jimmy's face in his hands. "Don't it make a difference if it's all I got left? What else do I have? I can't say I never stole anything. I can't say I was a saint. I can't talk about some good job I had."

Jimmy pushed Crab's hands away. "So don't say anything," he said, turning away. "Just be you and let me be me."

"I got to say something, son," Crab said softly. "You're all I got in this world that means anything to me. If you can't mean nothing to me then I don't have any meaning."

"That why you brought me down here?" Jimmy said. "All the way from Mama Jean's? So you can get some meaning to your life?"

A swarm of gnats flew around Crab's face and he stepped back and swatted at them.

"I wanted you to listen," Crab said, his voice rising. "I wanted you to listen and maybe hear something you wanted to hear."

"So say what you want to say," Jimmy said. He looked into Crab's face. He saw the tears running down Crab's dark cheeks, tears that mixed with sweat and glistened on his chin. "Go ahead."

They stood facing each other. Crab lifting his hands and searching for the words he thought he had known by heart. Jimmy searching his face for meaning beyond what he would say, knowing that he might not trust anything that was just words.

"Is it wrong if I don't know the words?" Crab asked. "Can't I just be your father?"

"You don't even know how to be a father!" Jimmy said.

The words had come tumbling out of Jimmy in a rush of anger that filled him and lifted his arms and clenched his hands into fists of a blind rage, and even as the rage surged within him it brought with it the clear and naked truth that Crab did not indeed know how to be a father, and that was the terrible knowledge that they shared.

"Here comes Miss Mackenzie's girl," Crab said, breaking the tension. His eyes went for a moment to Jimmy's face, and then down to the ground.

Jimmy turned and saw the girl running toward them. He turned back to Crab, and took a step toward him.

"Why don't you fix yourself up," Jimmy said.

Crab wiped his face with his shirt. Jimmy looked at him, then reached over and touched Crab's face where the tears and mucus had left a stain. Crab wiped the spot with his shirt.

"I'll go to California if you want," Jimmy said, trying to talk quickly. "Maybe you can get a job out there. Maybe I can even get a job out there."

"California's a long way," Crab said. "A long way."

The girl reached them, slowing as she ran, walking the last few steps. Jimmy saw her small bosom heaving against the dark blouse she wore, lifting the lace at the top.

"Mr. Rydell come back to the house," she said. She was speaking to Crab, but looking out the sides of her eyes at Jimmy. "Another car come, too. With some white men in it. Mama told me to tell you."

"She tell Rydell where I am?"

"She said she didn't know," the girl said. "Then she sent me to come the long way to tell you."

Crab looked up into the sky and exhaled slowly. The girl looked at him, then at Jimmy, as if she expected an answer. Her amber eyes caught the flat brightness of the sun and forever changed how Jimmy would think of his mother. The corners of her mouth moved into a smile that lasted for a heartbeat and then she turned and walked away.

"Who are the other men?" Jimmy asked.

"I don't know," Crab said. "Miss Mackenzie must think it's the police or she wouldn't have sent the girl."

"What you going to do?"

"Get on down to the rail crossing," Crab said. "Maybe get a freight heading out West. Give me some time to do some thinking. You give me some time to get on a freight, then go back to Miss Mackenzie's. You got enough money to go back to Jean's?"

Jimmy looked away from Crab.

"You want to walk with me to the crossing?" Crab asked. He gestured the direction with his chin.

"That's it?" Jimmy asked. "Walk with you to the crossing?"

"Maybe we can think of something," Crab said.

"Like what?"

Crab didn't have an answer.

The heat of the day bore down on them, wrapped itself around their shoulders, and pushed toward the earth that hardened as they moved away from the creek toward the crossing. The heat slowed Jimmy's steps, until he was walking in an uneasy rhythm with Crab. He wanted to stop, to forget where he was going, to forget everything except the search, the mining for reasons for these moments.

He wanted to grow up, to be grown, to have a mind that had answers where his own mind had questions. He didn't look at Crab, but knew he was there from the tug of the barbed wire silence strung between them. His heart beat quickly, as if he had been running, and he felt as if he had been running, running to catch the shadow of what could have been.

"It don't look like it used to," Crab said when they had reached the crossing.

"This ain't it?"

"It looks bigger," Crab said. The ground that had been soft and dark near the river was hard and light. There was a coarse grass that grew almost waist high that stretched from the small rise they had just crossed to the crossing itself. "Those buildings weren't there the last time. . . ."

The last time he was here, Crab was thinking, had been such a long time before. The low buildings with their corrugated roofs hadn't been there, or the giant cranes that stood like great mechanical insects on the far side of the water tower.

"I gotta go," Crab said.

"So go," Jimmy answered. There was as much anger as hurt in his throat, enough to choke him and turn him away from any dream he had ever had.

So go. What else was there to say? There wasn't time enough or world enough to piece together their prison dreams.

Jimmy felt Crab's hand squeeze his shoulder and leave, the fingers lingering a heartbeat after the palm, moving away just as Jimmy lifted his shoulder in response.

So go.

He looked down at the ground, and then up at the man walking away from his life. He watched the herky-jerky movement of his shoulders and knew that his legs were stiff. He remembered the aspirin and for a moment thought of running after him to remind him to get some more as soon as he had the chance. The moment passed.

And then he saw the car move from behind the crane. It stopped and two men got out, one on either side. One was in uniform, the other in civilian clothing.

Jimmy looked toward Crab. He had seen them, too. He was standing still, watching them. One of the men went slowly to the backseat of the car and pulled a shotgun through the window. Then they waved at Crab.

Crab turned and started to run. The two men got into the car and started across the field after him.

"Crab!" Jimmy called to him. "Watch out!"

Jimmy felt himself running, not toward Crab but in the same direction, his arms moving as Crab's were moving. The police car covered the ground and went between Crab and the crossing. Crab turned, disappeared for a moment in the high grass, then reappeared, running back toward the creek. The two men were out of the car and racing toward him. Then, as quickly as Crab had started, had run, had sprinted through the grass, he stopped.

The policemen stopped and looked at him. The

one with the rifle lifted it, and Jimmy's eyes sped to Crab. Crab was near a light pole, bent over, hands on his knees, his chest heaving.

"Lie down on the ground with your hands behind your head!" the policeman with the rifle called out.

Crab lifted his head and looked toward Jimmy. Jimmy motioned for him to lie down before the policeman shot him. Crab straightened up, leaned against the pole, and waved his hand.

Jimmy wasn't sure if Crab had beckoned toward him or the policeman but he started toward him. The policeman looked at him, then toward Crab. Crab was coughing, hanging onto the pole. By the time they reached him he was lying on the ground, his legs drawn up to his chest, his arms shaking.

"Get down on the ground with him!" the heavier of the two policemen called to Jimmy.

"No! It's just a kid!" the other one said as he walked over and looked at Crab. He bent down and patted Crab's pockets, then stood up and started talking into the radio he carried.

Crab was trying to shield his face from the sun. Jimmy looked at his face. It was calm as he turned and tried to straighten his legs.

"Hey, man" — he took a deep breath — "I'm sorry."

"I know, Daddy," Jimmy said. "I know."

A pigeon landed on the window ledge, lifted its wings twice, and then settled down in the corner of the frame. The window was closed, and the only thing that Jimmy could see from where he sat was another hospital building. On the bed Crab's right leg was bent under the sheet, the knee looking like the top of a small mountain. Jimmy had seen the policeman put the leg cuffs on Crab's left ankle and lock it to the foot of the bed. Crab's eyes were closed. It was not that he was asleep, but that his eyes were closed somewhere between knowing what went on around him and not knowing. Sometimes his legs would move, the right one would straighten, the left one would move against the chain.

"We have turkey and mashed potatoes." The black orderly who carried the tray in and set it on the white hospital table glanced at Jimmy. "You like ice cream? We got ice cream and Jell-O."

The policeman looked in, then told the orderly to take the knife on the tray.

"How he gonna eat the turkey?" the black man asked and left the room.

"You hear what I told you?" the policeman followed the orderly out of the room.

Jimmy was hungry. He hadn't eaten since they had left the crossing, since the policemen had put Crab in the back of the police car and brought him to the hospital. He looked at the potatoes, pushed them into a pile, and made a hole in the middle of them.

It was Crab's food. Crab's potatoes and turkey and creamed corn and ice cream. It was his little cup of fruit salad and his drink in a paper cup.

It was Sunday; Miss Mackenzie and Jesse had been there earlier and had left for church, promising to return.

"I'm going to get some prayers started for him," Miss Mackenzie had said. "What God can't do ain't worth doing. You just keep that in mind. We're going to be back before tonight, soon as Mr. Logan can get us over here."

He had nodded and told them that he would be all right. Soon after they had left Crab had awakened and was in pain. He had looked around the room, had tried to speak to Jimmy, and had settled for a nod. He looked around him, trying to figure out what was happening to him. They had put a tube into his side to drain liquids from his lungs, and the machine hummed quietly in the corner. He nodded to it, and Jimmy repeated what the nurse had told him.

"Get the nurse," he had said.

Jimmy thought that he didn't want to have the machine on, or the tube that went under the bandage and into his side, but when the nurse came in he told her that he couldn't take the pain. She didn't speak but left and came back with two pills and water.

Crab started talking to him after a while, moving his mouth in a funny way, so that his lips seemed too thin to cover his teeth.

"You got to be — you know — good and everything," he said. "You don't want to live like — well, sometimes things don't go right and . . ." His voice trailed off.

"Why don't you get some rest?" Jimmy said.

"So sometimes you think" — Crab went on — "that things work this way or that. That's what — if you go downtown — "

Jimmy saw Crab's eyes half closed and felt his own chest heaving. He had left the room and went down to the nurse's station, trying not to panic, not to run.

"He's acting funny," he had said.

The nurse had followed him back to the room and the policeman had put down his magazine to go with them. The nurse picked up Crab's wrist and felt the pulse.

"He's just sleeping," she said. "He needs to sleep."

What Jimmy told himself was that he was waiting for Miss Mackenzie. He imagined her praying in the church. He flattened the potatoes and put the fork down. On the ledge the pigeon was still huddled in the corner, its feathers puffed, its head tucked into its puffed breast.

Crab exhaled heavily and Jimmy turned toward him. He stirred and Jimmy went to the side of the bed and took his hand. He opened his eyes, just for a moment, and his mouth widened into what could have been a smile. Jimmy smiled even as the moment of warmth that had filled Crab's face disappeared.

"How you doing?" Jimmy asked him.

He was quiet again, the hand limp in Jimmy's. Jimmy looked at the earth-brown head against the white pillow, the color drained from its face, the mouth slightly open, the eyes almost closed but not quite so that he could see the dark round edge of the pupils.

"Crab?" he called. "Crab?"

This time he did not go all the way down the hall to the nurse's station but waited until she looked up and saw him.

The woman looked away for a minute, then sighed and went down the hall again. The policeman was looking through the yellow pages. When the nurse came back down the hall she touched Jimmy on the shoulder and said that he could wait for his family in the doctor's office if he wanted.

It rained the day of the funeral. The funeral was held at a church called New Bethel and afterwards they had made the short trip to a small cemetery where the graves were laid out in uneven rows and everybody sat on wooden chairs while a heavy woman sang "Precious Lord." He had spoken to Mama Jean on the phone but she couldn't come; she had used all her money to get a ticket for him to come back to New York.

"I'm real sorry, baby," she had said. "I really am."

Afterwards Miss Mackenzie and Jesse rode with him in Mr. Logan's car to the Memphis train station. Everybody told him how sorry they were. Jesse asked him if he was ever coming back to Marion, and he said no.

"I didn't think so," she said.

All the way home on the train Jimmy kept thinking about the moment in the hospital when Crab had stirred and might have smiled at him. Jimmy wanted it to have been a smile, a smile that had come because they had shared something, had been together for those few last moments. But sometimes, as the train raced through small towns, old buildings huddled around the stations, he felt that Crab had not been smiling, but had laughed at his concern because he was a kid and Crab was a man. Jimmy's thoughts went back and forth, between the smile and the laugh. It wouldn't have been bad if it had been a laugh, if Crab had just found again how young Jimmy was, and had laughed, as best he could, before death caught him unaware. It would have been better if it had been a smile.

Jimmy thought about his having a child. It seemed so far off, like something that could never happen, but somehow would. He thought about what he would do with the child if it were a boy. He wouldn't know much about getting money to buy food for him, or what things to tell him to do except to be good and not to get into trouble. But he would tell him all the secrets he knew, looking right into his eyes and telling him nothing but the truth so that every time they were together they would know things about each other. That way there would be a connection, he thought, something that would be there even when they weren't together. He would know just how he was like his son, and how they were different, and where their souls touched and where they didn't. He knew if he ever had a son he would have to do it right away, and all the time, because sooner or later there wouldn't be enough days left to fit the meaning in.

When he got off the train he looked around to see if Mama Jean was there, even though she had told him she would be working. He got the escalator up into the lobby of Pennsylvania Station, through a crowd of businessmen headed past the information booth to another gate. A tall, balding man dropped his attaché case, which opened and sent papers all over the tiled floor. Jimmy stopped while the man scooped the papers up, shoved them back into the case, and ran on.

There were kids standing around a sports car, and Jimmy looked at the clock to see if they should have been out of school. He looked through his pockets, found his token money, and headed for the subway and home.